Ultramarine
stories

Lucy Weldon

Best wishes

Lucy Weldon

LEAF BY LEAF

Published by Leaf by Leaf
an imprint of Cinnamon Press,
Office 49019, PO Box 92, Cardiff, CF11 1NB
www.cinnamonpress.com
The right of Lucy Weldon to be identified as author of this work has been
asserted by her in accordance with the Copyright, Designs and Patent Act,
1988. © 2023 Lucy Weldon.
Print Edition ISBN 978-1-78864-964-3
British Library Cataloguing in Publication Data. A CIP record for this
book can be obtained from the British Library.
Designed and typeset in Adobe Caslon Pro by Cinnamon Press.
Cover design by Adam Craig © Adam Craig

Cinnamon Press is represented by Inpress.

Contents

For my parents
AHW and BGWW

Foreword

It is rare that a story collection weaves its threads through so many varied corners of the world—Jakarta, Tel Aviv, Hong Kong, Denmark, Arizona, East Africa—and leaves the reader with an overarching sense of the vulnerability of humanity in all its mutable forms.

Lucy Weldon tackles the immensely difficult task of addressing a veteran's PTSD, the ever-pervasive threat of war in Israel, women's rights, the plight of immigrants—with an especially moving portrait of an Arizonian outlier who defies the system and finds a poetically heroic way to touch the lives of the immigrants he meets—and the deep and abiding grief of a woman drowning in an unfulfilling marriage who has just lost her mother.

There is the stark brutality of rape that renders an immigrant woman mute. There is love lost and love found within these stories. When it is found the magic of discovery is transcendent. And when it is lost there grows within the reader an acute mourning that Weldon brings forth with her exquisite and emotionally astute prose.

So staggering is the breadth and scope of Weldon's focus that the reader is moved by the author's own humanity in having taken on so much, given so much with prose that is almost defiantly unique in its rhythm, timbre and cadence, and its very clearly beating heart. The works of Nobel laureate, Kazuo Ishiguro, come to mind in the reading of this collection. As to why, one must look again to the humanity in each of the stories, to the empathy elicited in the reader by one who understands the power of human kindness.

The collection's title story—*Ultramarine*—gives us, arguably, one of the most sympathetic male characters in contemporary prose: the nerdy husband John whose wit and subsequent heroism in the face of near-certain death endears the reader for all time. There is frequently the fresh and unexpected phrase, an especially keen insight given with a quick brushstroke, and all of it achieved so deftly that one is moved to give a standing ovation when the final story is done. And, yes, to weep.

Lorian Hemingway, February 2023.

Lorian Hemingway is the critically acclaimed author of *Walking Into the River, Walk on Water,* and *A World Turned Over.* Ms. Hemingway is the director and final judge of the Lorian Hemingway Short Story Competition.

Ultramarine
stories

A thousand paper cranes

The Lazy Susan is turning. Anneka watches. Guests' fingertips spin it clockwise then anticlockwise, slowly, politely, waiting for each serving spoon to be placed back. The chicken satay Madura on thin bamboo skewers shines with caramelised palm sugar. The white rice waits like perfectly wrapped parcels. The aromas of garlic, galangal and chilli from the beef rendang hover. Candles on the round teak table flicker under the cool of the air conditioning.

It's yet another dinner party in Jakarta, Anneka thinks. There's been no let up. Tonight, she's been caught by the invisible tripwire of grief. She's on the outside looking in. That's what grief does, it turns you inside out. It pushes and pulls you. Anneka scans the guests. She counts. Eight is the perfect number. Snippets of lively conversation reach her. The dinner party is going well. Across the table is Alexander. Their age difference has crept up on them. Life has crept up on them. Who is he? She's been wondering that for a while now. Who are they? Once a couple, now strangers. It has nothing to do with her mother's death. Grief's making things clearer. Not cloudier. She's sure of that.

Everyone laughs at something Alexander says. Something about the rain that will come soon. Typical. It's always Alexander in the spotlight. Always right, always master and commander. But not of her. She still feels marooned after her mother's unexpected death three months ago. It's not about moving on. She keeps telling him that. And he keeps giving her books, sending her links to articles on grief. Podcasts!

The Lazy Susan has stopped. Alexander moves it with short staccato movements to get her attention. It's a hint. No, an instruction. Eat! Anneka refuses to meet his gaze. She's not hungry. All she wants is to curl up on the sofa with something comforting like soto ayam, chicken soup. She told him she's finding it hard to talk to new people at the moment. Don't sit me by anyone I don't know, she had said when he'd come home and told her about the dinner party. So many things she doesn't want to get into like how are you enjoying Jakarta, Anneka? A bit different from your last posting in Brussels! Alexander thinks it will be good for her to meet new people. If only he knew what was good for me.

She turns and looks at her neighbour. He's someone Alexander has met through Lili. What's his name? Pedro? Pietro? No. It's a much older sounding name. Piotr. That's it. Alexander introduced him when he arrived. Across the table, Anneka sees Rania, her

Egyptian friend, no longer fresh from the Arab Spring. Rania's stabbing the air with her fork, just above her plate filled with food. She's talking about the importance of educating women. A few of Rania's words drift across the table. Then the birth rate would drop. Look at Italy, for goodness' sake!

There's a thud. Otto has smacked his hand down to make a point to Lili. The silver cutlery jangles, forks jostling with knives. Anneka watches the beer as it moves up the side of Otto's glass. It happens in slow motion like a wave hitting a sea wall, like travelling liquid gold. She watches as it reaches the lip of the glass and then falls back. Otto's hand steadies it with an apologetic glance at the others. He can't keep off the topic of zoonotic diseases. It's his hobby horse. It's *the* discussion these days since the global pandemic.

Alexander says something about hoping that Otto has stamina. It'll be a long race. The fine balance between economic growth and the protection of the natural world. Ah, the pragmatic Alexander. Anneka glances at her husband. He's chatting to Lili. At home, in the security of his own house, away from the demands of diplomatic work, he can say exactly, almost exactly, what he likes. Lucky him, Anneka thinks. If she says what she's really thinking, she might bring the dinner party shebang to an embarrassing end. She checks herself. Shifts her position in her chair, trying to shake off these thoughts. Beside her, Andres is half out of his seat. He reminds her of Hugo, her younger brother, when he was a small boy and had a bug in a matchbox. Look at me! Look at me! Andres has the attention of the whole table.

'Did anyone know that there have been four earthquakes this month? Four, here in Jakarta! Did anyone notice?' he says.

Everyone shrugs. No one's noticed or even felt the tremors. Like most people living with the constant threat of natural disaster, they're a mixture of fatalism, optimism and naivety. In other words, they carry on as normal.

'When my time's up, it's up!' Lili says.

Everyone agrees with Lili, but Anneka doesn't. She notices the tremors. They usually come in the middle of the night from somewhere deep down in the Earth's crust. Somehow, they reach her. She's never mentioned this to Alexander. He's always been too busy, caught up in the latest diplomatic crisis. But the tremors find her, lying in her bed when she can't sleep. And sleep has eluded her these past months. There are times when she doesn't feel sane. In the dark, it's worse.

'And what if Gunung Tambora does its thing again? The biggest volcanic eruption in history. We're sitting on the Ring of Fire. Here in this dining room. It's a time bomb ticking away,' Andres says, enacting the explosion with arms flaying in the air.

At the mention of volcanoes, Anneka pictures the view outside the aeroplane window when she flies over Java. It's a dreamy fairy-tale illustration with perfect conical volcanic tops that poke through white cotton-wool clouds, vents that release twirling and trailing plumes of smoke. Is the smoke a signal, a message about our world, in a mysterious unspoken language?

Anneka notices Mitsuko and Piotr are having their own conversation. She sits back and listens in. She picks up the threads. Mitsuko is talking about fundamentalist Islam and whether it's a brake on progress, whatever that means. Mitsuko puts air quotes around those last few words. Piotr is folding a piece of paper in front of him. Anneka watches his hands and fingers as they neatly make creases. She wonders what he's making. It's been a long time since she's done origami. It was a childhood favourite. He folds the paper, each corner meeting at the centre of the square.

'But what about in Japan? Why does your country only allow male heirs to accede to the Chrysanthemum throne?' Piotr says. 'Isn't that a brake on progress?'

Piotr puts the last three words in air quotes. He's grinning. Anneka smiles. She likes his playful way. He obviously isn't a fan of air quotes and knows that an argument is rarely binary. Piotr turns the paper over and repeats the folds, taking the corners again back to the centre.

Ah, says Anneka to herself. She knows what he's making. Her mother taught it to her. She remembers its Dutch name, zoutvaatje. Salt cellar is the translation in English. Piotr finishes and takes out a pen. He covers what he's writing with his left arm, blocking Anneka's view. She can only see the top of his pen moving. Mitsuko tells him the latest on the Japanese royal family and how there's no sign of modernisation.

Piotr clicks his pen closed, picks up the origami game and slips his thumbs and index fingers into the corner pockets. He says something to Mitsuko and slowly turns his body to face Anneka. 'Would you like your fortune told?'

Ah, the fortune telling game, Anneka says to herself. That's its other name in English.

Piotr asks the question again. She shakes her head.

'I'm sure Mitsuko wants to play,' she says.

'But I want to tell your fortune, Annie,' Piotr says.

Annie? He's changed her name already! Her mother always called her Annie. There's a split second when Anneka feels tempted but she shakes her head again. Piotr glances at her. He puts the fortune telling game on the table. He places his finger to his lips. There's a dance of lights in his pale blue eyes, more than the normal catchlights. A conspiracy is building between them that only they are part of. She can feel it. He takes another piece of paper. He starts to make folds.

Piotr has drawn her into the evening. It's as if he's dropped down a thick sturdy rope and is pulling her out of a dark hole. He nudges her with his elbow. Accidentally but gently. It's the slightest of touches. She's raw. She can feel his skin through the layers of her skin, right down to the bone. She slides the fortune telling game into her pocket. Piotr's arm is alongside hers on the table. There's a wafer-thin gap between them. She feels warmth radiating from his arm, through his shirt. Everything she hears and feels has been amplified. It's what life is like these days.

Anneka looks at what he's now making. It's full of folds and creases, nothing like the fortune telling game.

'Almost there,' Piotr says.

But he doesn't look up as he continues to make more

and more tiny folds, running his fingers along the minute creases. Anneka watches.

Finally, Piotr stops and holds his creation up. 'There!'

Anneka stares at the paper object in the palm of his hand.

'It's a Japanese crane, a red crane that lives on the island of Hokkaido. They're very rare,' he says. 'They mate for life and dance for each other. So magical, don't you think?' The origami crane wobbles on Piotr's extended hand. 'The saying goes that if I make you a thousand of these, the Gods will look down favourably and grant you happiness and prosperity.'

Piotr picks the crane up and holds it by the wing with his fingertips. Anneka's hand goes out towards the paper bird. There's a split second when they're both holding the crane.

'So, here's the first,' Piotr says.

Anneka is lost for words. She's usually the host that can segue into any conversation, any topic, with any person. She can hear Alexander. His voice is above everyone else's. The paper crane is still in her hand. She places it carefully onto her lap. She thinks of the fortune telling game in her pocket. She thinks about the questions and the answers Piotr has written. She knows they're only ever to do with love, money and chance. Funny how even as children, we all write the same questions, she says to herself. It's as if we've always known what matters.

Piotr turns and joins Mitsuko's conversation with Otto. They're talking about how Jakarta is one of the fastest sinking cities in the world. How the flimsy sea walls can't hold back the rising Java Sea. Anneka leans forwards. She spins the Lazy Susan slowly. Across the table, Alexander stops talking. She can sense him looking at her. She picks up a spoon and starts to fill her plate. All of a sudden, she's hungry. She must eat. Out of the corner of her eye, she spots something on the tablecloth beside her. Another paper crane! Piotr's hand slides it closer to her.

'Here's your second one,' he whispers.

Anneka rests the spoon. This time, she picks up the crane and cups it in both hands. She can feel its edges and corners, its sharp beak, neck, its wings, its long tail. She can feel it nestling there like a fragile injured bird. She sits back in her chair.

'Eat! Eat! And let's have a coffee and dessert before the rain comes,' Alexander says.

The next day, Anneka leaves the house. She's running late. She's skipped breakfast to try and make up the time. She gets into the back of the waiting car. Andres's words were going round and round in her head about the Ring of Fire and volcanoes; then Otto and Mitsuko talking about Jakarta sinking. When she finally got to sleep, it was the early hours of the morning. She didn't hear the alarm. Alexander is long gone.

She needs to decide about her mother's legacy and then talk to Hugo. She'll call him soon. He's waiting. So's Lili. She messages Lili to say she's running late. Lili responds immediately telling her not to come. *We can meet another day. There's always another day. Boleh*, Anneka messages back in Bahasa. Can. She needs to get out of the house and away from all the preparations for tonight. She works out how long it will take to get to Kedoya and then back again. There's never a quiet time of day or night in Jakarta.

Anneka glances up to the sky out of the car window. There was a lot of talk about rain last night. Rainy season, it can change the day completely. It can ruin a day too. If it rains today, *when* it rains, Anneka knows she mustn't get caught out. She checks the time on her watch. It's risky, given how late she's left it now. She's regretting her decision, as the car pulls away from the house and joins the steady crawl of traffic on the main road. She thinks back to last night. They were standing at the front door, Lili, herself and Alexander. Lili said to come and see what she does with her charity. They could talk about it. Then she and Alexander had another argument over her mother's legacy. Watch out for the slumlords, he'd said, before saying, well, go if you want, as long as you're back in time. You know what's in the diary. Alexander has put the dinner party in red ink in her diary. Another dinner party. A work one, full of officials and protocols. Don't be late, Anneka, very important. Very important is underlined three times. He's put a smiley emoji by it. That means please in Alexander speak.

Travelling through the city to Kedoya, Anneka gazes at the passing street scenes. The putting on a brave face last night has tired her. The façade of cheerfulness, the show must go on, the avoidance and the busyness that masks the inner reality have taken their toll. But Piotr and his conversation have lingered. She thinks of him, the teasing origami game and the paper cranes he made for her. Her mother's legacy has been weighing on her mind too. She hopes she can sort it out today when she meets Lili. Alexander's made his view clear. As always. She gets her book out. She's still got at least another half an hour to go, if she's lucky.

The car finally comes to a standstill. Anneka checks her watch. She calculates again how much time she has before she has to be home, to keep the peace. Three hours. Anneka searches through the busy street for Lili. She spots her and gets out of the car. She walks to where her friend is standing by the railway line that runs past the slum.

'You made it, Anneka! Let's go,' Lili says. 'Let's cross over. Quick before the train comes.'

Lili skips across the first pair of tracks, then walks through the gravel middle that separates it from the next pair. Anneka notices Lili does this without looking. But Anneka pauses. She's listening for the suburban trains that come in and out of Jakarta. They pass right where she's standing. Tentatively, Anneka follows Lili across the double set of tracks. She reads the large signs in red and white, Dilarang! Dilarang! She knows what the word means. It's an unheeded message. A warning. Be careful! People cross the tracks. Children are even playing on them. There's hustle and bustle.

She catches up with Lili on the other side. A young girl on a pink bicycle comes riding alongside them, sounding her bell. The bike has coloured pennants hanging from the handlebars. They're droopy with the slow pace of the peddling. Lili greets the child.

'This is Dewi,' Lili says. 'You can tell it's been her birthday, can't you? Her brother is sick. He's one of the children we're helping through the charity.'

The two women watch Dewi cycle away.

'You see, Anneka,' Lili says. 'It's normal life. People are getting up to work, having a shit, washing from a bucket, going to school, heading to work, coming home, cooking, doing homework, eating and sleeping. Just like you and me.'

No one looks at Anneka. They're used to foreigners, tourists, coming to their community. Slum tourism they call it these days. Anneka's not sure what she thinks of it. It's yet another dinner party conversation in Jakarta she's had and heard. Is it voyeurism? Exploitation? Cultural exchange? A fast way to earn a rupiah. Actually, earn a US dollar, that's the currency that matters. Anneka glances at the low sky. It's dark grey. Today, the humidity's extreme. She follows Lili, walking parallel to the tracks. Men on motorbikes carve carefully around her. A popsicle seller catches Anneka's eye.

'That means the rain will come. The women always know,' Lili says, pointing to the empty washing lines that link the houses. 'And the women always know who needs help. They know what's going on. We call them the gossip women. They're key to the charity.'

Their conversation's interrupted. Anneka feels the ground rumble. She thinks of Andres and his talk about tremors and earthquakes. There's a blast of a horn. Nobody looks up except her. She and Lili are still standing on the side of the railway track. There's nowhere for her to go except against the side of the corrugated iron housing. The train comes like a steel monster. Up close, it's bigger, more lethal than she could ever imagine. The train hurtles pass. She counts the carriages. It's a passenger train, not a freight train, as if that matters.

'It's okay, it's okay, Anneka. The trains come all the time. There's no need to be frightened. You just get used to it,' Lili says, putting an arm around Anneka. 'Come on, I'll show you around before you have to leave. It won't take too long.'

Anneka hears her phone ringing. She takes it out. It's Alexander.

'Where are you?' he says.

'You know where I am. I'm in Kedoya,' Anneka says, turning away from Lili.

'You were fast asleep so I left you a message. On the hall table. To say don't go to Kedoya,' he says. 'The rain's coming for sure.'

Alexander must have called the house to speak to her. They'd have told him when she had left. And now he's worried about the rain and traffic and whether she'll be home in time. She doesn't want to row in front of Lili. She doesn't want a row at all. She looks at the scene in front of her and remembers Lili's words about how life just goes on here. She's made a decision. She thinks back to the fortune telling game. How the questions are always about love, chance and money. Well, she's answered this one about money. She has. She'll talk to Hugo. She'll talk more to Lili. They can all do a video call and if Hugo really wants a virtual slum tour, she can ask Lili to do that.

'Sorry, Lili. You know what it's like,' Anneka says as she ends the call.

She wants to say, you know what Alexander is like. She points to the sky. Lili hugs her.

'I'll call you tomorrow. And all this,' Lili waves her arm in the direction of the railway tracks, 'isn't going anywhere. But you need to go home, I can tell.'

Anneka gets back into the waiting car. She shivers with the blast of icy air conditioning. There's another message from Alexander. The number of messages correlates to how anxious he's feeling about tonight's dinner. The car engine starts. She waves at Lili who is already walking away, talking on the phone. And sends a message to Alexander.

On my way. Hope you get the pawang hujan to sort the rain out.

The pawang hujan is the rain master. Business is brisk in the rainy season. It's another dinner party staple, discussing whether these practitioners of magic actually work. Are they just quackery, their fasting, their prayers and meditating, their offerings to the spirits? Anneka doesn't think so. Alexander is more sceptical but he'll pull out all the stops for tonight. The sky's threatening. The single sheet of grey air above is waiting to download. When it rains, the rain will be heavy. The roads will become impassable in minutes. She should have listened to Alexander. The Ciliwung River will swell. She asks the weather Gods to be kind and benevolent. But it's like the volcanoes and earthquakes.

There's nothing she can do about it.

A motorbike passes by the car, along the inside. It's one of dozens and dozens that swarm and cluster around her. She sees a large polystyrene box strapped to the seat behind the driver. It's got black lettering on it. Norway Salmon Trondheim, it says. Ah, just arrived. Farmed salmon, shipped across the world, ready for the six-star hotels and European tourists who want to feel at home. Economic equations start to form in Anneka's head, how much each airfreighted piece of Norwegian farmed salmon would cost in an international restaurant. She hopes salmon isn't on the menu tonight. What the hell is wrong with pecel lele? She salivates at the thought of spicy catfish with a heaty sambal.

The rain starts. It's only a sputter. Large drops tap the glass. The car wipers go on. Traffic slows. Motorbikes pull over. Riders cover up with poncho-style waterproofs. Everyone knows what's coming. Anneka catches the eye of her driver in the mirror. He shrugs. There's nothing he can do. His phone rings.

'Boleh. Boleh,' he says. Can. Can.

She listens. She knows enough Bahasa to understand he's now giving directions to the caller. Opening her book, she reads. It's going to be a crawl home. Should she warn Alexander she's going to be late? It's now mid-afternoon. If she's not back by five, he'll be panicking. But things could turn on a dime. She shakes her head. They won't. Not with the rain that's about to unleash itself. She leans her head against the window, exhausted by the heat and her visit to Kedoya. That train! She closes her eyes. She can't concentrate enough to read.

The car comes to a standstill. A knock on the car window, right by her ear, makes her jump. Through the tinted glass, she sees a man with a crash helmet covering his face. It's the Norwegian Salmon rider, she says to herself. Maybe he thinks she's been chasing him like a cat after a mouse through Jakarta. She looks away. The man knocks again. He gives her the signal to wind down the window. She opens it. He says something. His words are muffled by the helmet. Then she hears what he's saying. He's saying her friend's name.

'Lili called. She said you had to get home on time. She said with the rain you might be late.'

The man lifts his visor. She sees his eyes, crinkling at the corners. Somewhere in his helmet, he's smiling at her. His eyes are the palest of blue. He lifts up another helmet and offers it to her.

'Annie! Let's go. You can't sit in this traffic all day. Come with me. Quickly before the rain really comes.'

She knows who it is. His voice. She remembers his eyes from the night before, the catchlights and the extra lightness of them. Piotr opens her door. Anneka gets out of the car. She stands facing him. The traffic swarms and slides around them. They're like an island with streams of water rushing past. She takes the helmet from him quickly and puts it on, tying the strap tightly beneath her chin. The only way to cut through the traffic is on a motorbike.

'Take this. Put it on.' Piotr gives her a leather jacket.

The coolness and heaviness of the leather on her shoulders make her feel safe. Piotr is now back on the motorbike. He's manoeuvred it to the side of the road under a large ficus tree.

'Hurry, Annie. Quick. The rain's coming. Hold on to me. Tight.'

His voice is insistent, firm. On the bike, she closes her eyes. She feels it move left and right as Piotr carves his way through the traffic. She relaxes. There's nothing she can do. She just wants to leave, to escape, to stop suffocating in her gilded cage and to breathe, to breathe air, air that doesn't cloy and stick to her. And to sleep.

Anneka walks towards the house. Piotr has gone. The last few hours have been like a dream. The bike ride, the downpour forcing them to stop. They found a warung, a roadside food stall. They sat on tall red plastic stools as water pooled around their feet, eating her favourite pecel lele. And she talked. They both talked. Sometimes they had to shout above the rain. A rare leukaemia, she'd said when Piotr asked her how her mother had died. She talked about her mother as if she'd been bottled up and gagged for the past three months.

Piotr told her about his brother, Tomasz, his twin, who had died in a motorbike accident. 'Yeh, I know,' he'd said, reading her expression. 'But that's what makes me feel close to him. Riding on a motorbike. That's when I talk to him. You see, I never got the chance to say goodbye.'

That word. Chance, Anneka thinks to herself as she waits for the tall gates of the house to swing open for her. She checks the time. It's coming up for six o'clock. She knew she was going to be late. In the air, she can smell the citronella of the candles already lit along the paths. She lets her hand brush against plants that hang heavy with the afternoon rain. Her fingers trail over petals, strong and robust to withstand tropical downpours. She gives the front door a push and slips inside. The house is cool. Sounds and smells of cooking escape the kitchen. She quickly takes her shoes off and goes up the stairs two at a time feeling the smooth polished gleaming teak wood beneath her. She's been heard, seen. Invisible ears and eyes have registered her return. They'll tell Alexander.

As she enters the bedroom, Anneka sees her tangerine coloured dress already laid out on the bed. It's as long as the bed, stretching from the pillows to the foot end. Alexander calls it her lucky dress. It slips on and off easily, dropping to her ankles like a waterfall, in a single silky movement. But doing it up is another matter. She frowns. Why did he pick that dress tonight? Why did he pick a dress at all?

She checks her phone for messages. Her heart skips a beat. She tells herself to stop being silly. Piotr was only giving her a lift home. He just feels sorry for her. He's been in the same boat. And, in any case, Lili asked him to go and get her. That's what he'd said. Lili had called him from Kedoya as Anneka was leaving. She remembers that now. Anneka quickly types a message to Alexander. He'll be in his study. *I'm home. Come upstairs.* She undresses and jumps in the shower. She needs to clear her mind. She puts her head under the jet of water.

Running the palm of her hand down her arms and

legs, she cleans the sticky gritty coating of the city off her skin. The bedroom door opens. She finishes showering and dries. She goes back into the bedroom. Out of the window, the sun is sinking like a stone in the sky. It'll be dark soon.

'It's the buttons,' she says to Alexander, as she picks up the dress. 'I can never do them up.'

Alexander's sitting on the edge of the bed. He watches her get ready. 'Where've you been all afternoon? You didn't answer my messages.'

'Oh, I was with Lili. You know that.'

'I was worried about you. I got your text. I just thought you would be home much earlier. Rain in the afternoon messes up everything.'

'Ik ben niet van suiker!' Anneka says.

That's what her mother would always say to her about the rain. I'm not made of sugar! The rain doesn't do any harm. The dress is on her now, open and gaping around her shoulders, her back exposed. Alexander stands behind her. He kisses her neck. She can feel his warm breath. She shivers. She wants him to stop. He starts to do up the small silk-covered buttons on the dress, beginning at the base of her spine.

'Have you ever counted the buttons?'

'I have,' he says. 'Twenty-three.'

Anneka's surprised he knows.

'So, where else did you go?' Alexander asks again.

'I told you. Kedoya. Had a close encounter with a train.'

Anneka pauses.

'By the way, I think I've decided what to do with the

legacy.'

Anneka tenses. She can feel Alexander's fingers working up her back, across her spine, up to her neck. The buttons are all done. She waits for him to make a comment. He doesn't. He tells her he's going downstairs to wait for guests. She goes across to the dressing table and opens her jewellery box. The origami from last night's dinner party are inside. She picks up the fortune telling game, slides her index fingers and thumbs into the paper pockets. She chooses a number and counts it out, switching back and forwards. She selects a colour. Orange, of course! She spells the word out, and then unfolds the centre of the game to pick a question. What's Piotr written? But Anneka stops. Out of the window, she can see car headlights coming up the drive in the dark. The first guests are arriving. The umbrellas are at the ready. She puts the game back on her dressing table. Then, picking up her evening shoes, she walks quickly along the corridor towards the staircase.

'I hope the pawang hujan has done his job,' Alexander whispers to her as she reaches the bottom of the stairs.

He hardly looks at her as Anneka joins him at the front door. She quickly puts on some lipstick and checks herself in the mirror.

'Ready?' Alexander asks.

'Ready.'

The front door opens. They smile at tonight's guests who are walking up the path towards the house.

From the veranda chair, Anneka watches the palest edge of grey light in the sky emerge. The sun rises quickly in Jakarta. It was a late night. She'd slept better. Alexander's happier. His spark has returned. Relations are renewed. Anneka has even secured promises for funding for Lili's charity. They didn't eat Norwegian salmon for dinner. And the pawang hujan did his job. More rain came in the night but much later, long after the guests had gone.

The rain has cooled the early morning heat. The humidity is high, cloaking and muffling the sounds of the city. Mosquitoes hover. Anneka hears them. It's a seasonal hazard. Stagnant water is the culprit. Time to upturn buckets, flowerpots, anything that has caught the night rain. The Ciliwung River is full. Soon there'll be nowhere for the water to go except into the roads and people's houses.

A mosquito lands on her bare leg. Anneka is sitting so still she can feel its legs dragging against her skin. She quickly waves her hand through the air. The tiger mosquito brings dengue; they're black and leggy with white stripes. Females are the ones to watch out for, Alexander says. As if you can identify the female before it bites! Large fleshy waxy leaves from the frangipani tree drop, slowed by the humidity. A cockerel crows; the sound rips through the quiet of the garden, coming over the garden wall, from the small kampung below the house.

A white butterfly wafts in the humid air, like a tiny handkerchief, buoyed by moisture and a slight breeze. It dances over a brindled orchid. Rama, Anneka says, butterfly in Bahasa. She learnt that yesterday. Piotr also told her that butterflies are the spirits of dead people. She wishes it would land on her. It's been nearly a hundred days since her mother died. Here people believe the souls of the dead are still around. She wants to remember. She wants to give thanks. Selamatan. She learnt so much yesterday.

Anneka thinks of her mother. She lifts a strand of her hair and curls it behind her ear. It's a mannerism she inherited. She's becoming her mother. And she's glad. The Dutch saying is true. Zo moeder, zo dochter, like mother like daughter. Whether you like it or not, her mother would always say.

Voices drift from the hall. She hears Alexander. He's calling her. She calls back saying she's outside on the veranda. Moments later the screen door slides open. Alexander walks out, holding a large box.

'For you,' he says, putting it down on the table beside her.

Anneka thinks this is a peace offering, Alexander style.

'By the way, I have to go to Bali,' he says. 'Gunung Agung is kicking off. Andres and his rantings on volcanoes the other night have jinxed it. I have an island full of panicking tourists.'

Anneka's phone rings. Alexander waits for her to answer it. She doesn't recognise the number. She turns the phone over.

'Who's that? It's a bit early for someone to call. It might be important. You'd better answer it.'

'Oh, it's probably Lili. I'll call her back. Probably

wants to know if I've made a decision.'

Alexander frowns. He's about to say something but changes his mind. He goes back inside the house. It can't be, she says to herself. She dials her voicemail but there's no message. She looks at the box beside her on the table. Curling up on the rattan chair, she glances at the card. Her name's written on the envelope. It isn't Alexander's writing. The package is surprisingly light. Perhaps it's a joke, like once before, with plane tickets inside. She starts to unwrap the package, tearing off the paper. It's a white box, with a picture-frame lid of clear cellophane, filled with origami cranes. Multi-coloured, plain, some with patterns, stripes.

Anneka quickly takes the envelope. She tears it open. There's a small white card inside with a message written on it:

Annie, here is the first instalment of my gift of a thousand paper cranes. Piotr.

And out of nowhere, the morning rain comes like pebbles from the sky, hitting the roof and the edges of the veranda, splashing her bare legs. Anneka jumps up, grabs the box of paper cranes and runs inside. As soon as Alexander leaves, she'll go upstairs to their bedroom and find the fortune telling game. She watches the birds of paradise in the garden, their strong rigid stems unbowed under the heavy rain. I miss you. I really need to talk to you, she says to herself, as she hears Alexander calling her.

The sea between the lands

Marina feels flutterings in her stomach as she sits on the edge of the jetty. At the end of her fingers, there's a sharp tingling like blunt pinpricks. She shakes her hands to rid herself of the sensation. There mustn't be any distractions. This is how accidents happen. Is that what happened to Nannu? Was he distracted when he went spearfishing last Wednesday?

Before the dive, Marina's careful to keep the breathing preparation normal. She repeats the slow expansive exercise how she always has. How Nannu trained her. Exactly how they would prepare together. She's relaxing her diaphragm. Her rib cage. It's the breathe-up before she gets into the sea. Mustn't overdo it or she risks hyperventilating and blacking out in the water.

Time to go. She hasn't got long. Marina puts her fins on. She's always fidgety before a dive. But this morning, it's worse. The idea of looking for Nannu has taken root in her mind. Her grandfather's body still hasn't been found. She knows it's a risk diving on her own. It's against the rules, their rules. But she's only going to do a single dive. She doesn't want anyone to come with her. Not even Fabio. Leave it to the professionals, he keeps saying. He means the search and rescue team. She feels guilty. If she'd gone with Nannu last week, the accident wouldn't have happened. No one else thinks that. But she does.

As she readies herself, it feels familiar yet strange. It's always been Nannu, her diving buddy, sitting beside her, catching her eye, giving the hand signal, the nod, the tap on her shoulder. You go. You go first today. Your turn to lead. Pulling down her mask, Marina edges and shifts her weight. Time to go, she tells herself again. She tips forwards off the jetty. Her body slips like chiffon through the water, breaking open its surface momentarily.

Her strong arms pull her slowly beneath the shallow keels of Mermaid, Kaptan and Julie-Anne, small fishing boats anchored in the bay. Her long dark hair streams down her back. She pulses her legs, allowing her fins to do the work, sculpting her passage through the water, conserving her energy, being efficient with her body. She spots sea urchins tucked up in rock holes. Bubbles peel off from her fingers. A jellyfish passes her, trailing threads of silk. A small cloud of damsel fish shimmers at arm's length like drops of black ink. As she goes deeper, the light changes to long shafts. She pats her hip. Her knife is there. She'd already checked before the descent. Several times. Fishing nets are everywhere these days. Abandoned ghost nets too.

Nanna is now on her mind. Nanna's worrying about everyone and everything since the accident. It's understandable. She's already asked Marina not to dive anymore. Her grandmother was right to warn her about the weather today. The weather's unsettled like her mind. But why does Nanna have to keep going on about the migrants as well? Her grandmother had come over to the house yesterday. Have you seen the news? They're still coming. I don't know what they're thinking of, coming to our little island. Taking their children on these boats. Especially when the weather is so unpredictable.

As Marina descends in the water, she pictures her grandmother whipping the duster as she cleans. Flick, flick, flick, like a marker pen underlining her words. It's worse in summer! Look at Greece. Just like us. And the UK! Her grandfather had told Marina that their little island, Malta, has always had travellers from the beginning of time. They come like the wind from North Africa, bringing the sand from the Sahara. It's always been so.

Marina turns her body to go deeper. She's already passed five metres. She feels the temperature change on her hands. She's wearing her wet suit. Fabio will have seen it gone from the hangar in the garage. If she had told him what she was going to do, he would have tried to stop her. She sent him a message from the jetty to say where she was going, that she was only doing the one dive. To check an area again. Just one more time. Nannu's favourite spearfishing spot. Marina has a hunch. Hunting octopus at dusk was probably what

Nannu was doing, for his favourite dish, stuffat tal-qarnit, octopus stew.

The rock ledge is beneath her. She's now in the right spot. She scans quickly. Up, down, across. She knows the rock formations, how they jut, fall away behind into the darkness below, where the cracks are, the deep ones, the shallow ones, the hiding places for octopus. She moves quickly but carefully. The rocks always bring back memories of Nannu when he was teaching her how to swim deeper, preparing her for the first spear fishing dive together. Slim hipped, making silent gestures to her, tapping his dive watch, asking Marina for the hand signal that all was well. The thumb and forefinger in a circle, fingers up. And he would give the same signal back and turn, pushing off with his feet, the feet she has followed all her life. She does another sweep across the rock surfaces to check if his speargun is trapped in a crack, to say he was there. That something happened. But there's nothing.

Marina feels the current pulling her. This rocky area is her stopping point. No further. She must now think about her ascent. Stay calm or her body will use up oxygen too fast. Count. That's what Nannu always told her to do. She can hear his deep gravelly voice. She starts at thirty. She counts backwards. That's better. The counting is working. As it always does. She thinks of Lara and Stefano. They'll be at home. Awake. And Fabio will look after them today. She turns her body to a more vertical position. There's a small tightness in her chest which she must control. Any bigger, it'll take her over. She's feeling uncomfortable. An urge to breathe.

It's a natural body response. It's also a sign of carbon dioxide building up.

Stay calm, Marina says to herself as she travels slowly upwards to the sun-lit shelf of water above her head. All she wants to do is go straight there. But she can't. She still has to be careful. She equalises. She pauses. The last few metres can be the most dangerous. If she blacks out, she'll drown. She waits. She stops herself from looking up. Equalises again. Now it's safe. With her eyes closed, Marina breaks through the sea's surface. She feels the air on her skin. She gasps for breath. Her chest heaves. Her heart pumps in her ears. Her grandfather always warned her about the dangers of the sea. The sea will take us if we're not careful, Nannu always says. Always said.

It's the wind Marina notices straightaway. It's picked up, restless. She feels it on her face. It's building. The sea around her is whipped and flecked with white. Flipping on her back, she looks up at the sky, hips tilted to the wind-filled clouds above. She watches them scuttling past as her heartbeat and breathing settle. Her grandmother was right. The weather has shifted. It's August, too early for a Sirocco to bring its heat and sand from the Sahara. But the weather patterns are changing. That's what Fabio says. Watching the weather is part of his job in the Coast Guard.

Marina orientates herself to the shoreline, spotting the sun-crisped heads of wild fennel moving stiffly in the wind on their long stems, the salt trees that cluster on the limestone cliffs. She recognises Mermaid, Kaptan and Julie-Ann swinging on their moorings. She hears the clinking of anchor chains. Once the wind blows over a force five, the islanders abandon the sea and take refuge on land. And she must too. She starts to swim towards the jetty. Her grandmother's words are in her ears, what she always used to say to her as a child. Ejja, ilek biżżejjed fil-baħar u sar il-ħin. Marina, it's time to get out of the water.

Marina's done what she's needed to do. Nannu isn't there.

Maryam is curled on the rough concrete floor, knees to chin, as small as she can get. She's whispering to herself. 'Stay small so the wind can carry me across the sea like a grain of sand.' The small girl stops repeating her mother's words. She can't remember any more, except she does remember, back in the refugee camp, her mother saying that they weren't going to leave. Then she said they might be leaving, and then all of a sudden, they were leaving. The very next day. After that, there was no more talk, just quiet and the feeling that questions were not allowed.

'Ayeeyo says be careful what you say. Once you've said it, the words are out there like the spirits moving around. You can't take them back,' Maryam says quietly.

Maryam hasn't seen her grandmother for a long time. If she closes her eyes, she can see her by the stove preparing food, or bent over, sweeping. But she can't hear the crackle of her voice anymore. It's gone from her memory.

The girl looks around. The holding room is packed with people and smells. The smells remind her of the mountain of rubbish in the refugee camp before it was set alight. But Maryam is only half breathing, from the top of her chest. She's like a dog panting in the heat. It's worse than the game she used to play with her brothers when they held their breath until it hurt. Maryam and her mother have been waiting in the holding room for days. She's lost count how many. She feels her mother's hand touch her head. Her mother scoops Maryam towards her, guiding her head to the small narrow space between the soft underside of arm and ribs. There's a steeliness in her mother's long thin bony fingers, a strength.

'Hooyo,' Maryam says. 'Hooyo,' she whispers again, a little more fiercely.

Her mother's body shifts, a sign that tells Maryam she's been heard.

'I want to pee,' she says.

Her mother strokes her head. Maryam remembers when she stopped talking. It was after her mother was pulled off the lorry. Don't move! The men shouted at Maryam. They waved guns at her. Don't move, they kept on yelling. She waited and waited. No one spoke to her. Then her mother was brought back. The lorry driver snapped twigs. He lit a fire and made tea. Her mother held the cup. She didn't drink the tea. That's when she stopped talking.

A man's shouting. A small, rake-thin man stands at the far end of the room. He's by the wall where her mother wrote their names. The man reminds her of an animal, big eyes, long thin nose, always twitching. Sengi, Maryam says to herself as she looks at him.

41

Elephant shrew. That's what he looks like. Sengi's shouting over the heads of the women. She doesn't like his harsh voice, its sharpness, disturbing the quiet of the holding room. Her father never shouts like that. The man's waving his arms. He shouts again.

This time the women stir. They heave themselves up from the floor, picking up their sleeping babies. The babies' heads loll back, like dead weights. Toddlers cry, brightly coloured pacifiers hanging from their mouths, vibrating. Older children grab bundles and hands of younger children who can walk.

'It's time. It's time. If you want life jackets, you pay. If you want water, you pay. Pay now,' Sengi shouts.

Maryam sees something in his other hand. Money. She's seen paper money like that before. She remembers her father sitting on the edge of the bed, money box on his knees. He was counting notes like that. He put the paper money back in the tin box. He closed the lid, locking it, and placed it under the bed. She'd caught his eye for a split second, nothing longer, but it was enough to sense something was wrong.

Has her mother heard the question? Maryam looks up at her and tugs hard on her arm. She hasn't answered the man. She hasn't responded to Maryam's tug either. She must answer Sengi. If it's about money, it's important. That much Maryam knows. Her mother wraps her scarf tightly around her head and shoulders.

'Hooyo, do we need those?' Maryam says, pointing at the life jackets Sengi's holding up. 'The man has asked us.'

Sengi's now standing at the opened doors at the far

end of the holding room. She sees two women buying life jackets. He beckons the group. He shouts. Maryam and her mother move. The other women and children shuffle stiffly and slowly towards the doors. The girl hears women hushing and speaking in low tones to their children. Maryam holds her mother's hand tightly. She suddenly speaks.

'We're leaving now. Remember what I said to you, Maryam. Think of the fire, the fire at home. Think of Aabe, and your brothers. And you're not to cry,' her mother says, looking at the girl.

Maryam doesn't understand. She never cries. Her brothers say she never cries. Only if one of the goats gets lost or is taken at night. But that wasn't her fault. It's dark as they walk out of the holding room. Maryam's nostrils twitch at the smell. She knows where she is now. A long time ago, she was told that they would see the sea for the very first time, that they would cross the sea. The air's heavy and sticky. She licks her lips and tastes their saltiness. Touches the skin on her face. It's damp.

'Watch where you step,' her mother says.

The girl shuffles along the roughly made path. When she peers around the women in front of her, she sees a big wooden boat up ahead. Black tyres hang down from its side, rubbing the quay as the boat moves. Maryam hears a loud noise. She spots the gangway. It rears up and slams on the ground. Something's pushing it from below. She hears heavy, angry smacks of water against the concrete quay. The wooden boat and gangway are getting closer. She watches the women and children in

43

front of her, observing what they do. She notices how high the gangway is. How it keeps moving. How it's difficult to get up and get on to. It's her turn now. Her mother nudges her. Two taps and Maryam steps forward onto the gangway, but she stops, freezes. The gangway's jumping under her feet.

'It's too high,' she says. 'Too many people. I can't see.'

She used to be braver. She was the one who found the puff adder and told everyone. No one dared move until Aabe came with his long stick. But no one answers her now. There's a man in front of her, in front of the gangway, on the boat. He isn't Sengi. They look like brothers. The man says something but she can't understand him. He raises his arms up and claps his hands to get her attention. He calls her urgently. He wants me to jump. He'll catch me, she thinks.

Someone pushes her. Hard. She closes her eyes and falls forwards. The man's hands dig into Maryam as he catches her in her arm pits. It hurts. She screams out. She can't help herself. He puts her down on the deck of the boat. Her mother's behind her already. She quickly takes her hand once again and pulls her. Maryam wants to tell her mother about the hurt.

'Downstairs, downstairs. Women and children. Get down below.'

It's another man who shouts these instructions. Maryam can't see him. He's swallowed up by the women and the children. She follows the movement of dark shapes. It's like being in a tunnel. Following blindly, she steps down, holding her hands out in case she falls.

'Sit. Sit and wait down there. Down below. We wait until the captain gives his orders,' the man says.

The women and children huddle on the floor of the boat, on laps, on the feet of their mothers. The air's drenched with the smell of rotten fish. Maryam wants to block her nose, her ears, her mouth. She turns to her mother.

'Hooyo, how long…'

Her mother squeezes her hand.

'Hooyo, that hurts. You're hurting my hand.'

There are thumps on the deck above their heads. It could be men now boarding. Is it you, Aabe? My brothers? She hopes so, but she isn't sure. Leaning her head into her mother's body, Maryam closes her eyes, wriggling to find a space to fit into. Her mother moves and strokes the girl's head. She likes that. It helps her forget. She tries to get comfortable. Turning her face, she presses into her mother's clothes, shifting and shifting again. But there's no place to go.

The sound of engines silences the women. The girl hears clanking. The smell of diesel floods the cavity below decks. There's a ripple of movement as women put scarves and sleeves up to their mouths. Maryam's mother draws her daughter's face tightly into her body. But Maryam pulls away. She can't breathe. With her eyes closed, she listens to the noise of the engines. It sounds like the lorries they have travelled in. It smells like them too. Maryam wriggles to free her hands. Puts her thumbs in her ears and curls up tightly.

'Hooyo says stay small so the wind can carry me across the sea like a grain of sand,' she whispers to herself.

The boat moves. Maryam rocks with the motion as it leaves the quay. She falls asleep. She doesn't know for how long, but long enough for her to drool down her chin, which she wipes with her scarf when she wakes. She's groggy and damp. She puts her hand up to her face and wiggles her fingers. But she can't see them. Alert now, she blinks quickly to adjust to the dark. Be like a fruit bat, Aabe always says. Use your eyes and your ears. Listen. Listen. There's been a change. It takes her a few seconds to work out what's different. It's easy. Maryam listens to the boat creak and groan, rolling with the waves. The mechanical pump has stopped banging.

'Hooyo, Hooyo,' she whispers.

But her mother doesn't stir. Maryam feels her mother's breath moving in and out of her body. She's lying against her, listening. She feels the movement of the boat. She hears the creaking of wood. Does anyone else think something is different? She lifts her head off her mother's hip, her eyes peeking out from the scarf tied around her face. There are footsteps and the sound of running on the deck above. Is it Aabe? My brothers? They would come below. They would come if there was something wrong. Maryam hears a hammering of metal on metal. The low dulled tone of the men's voices comes through into the hold. The hammering stops. The boat's rhythm is now erratic, uneven, rocking as if being pushed hard by something.

The women wake. The hatch opens. The sound of the sea whooshes down into the hold. A man's voice shouts above the noise. He shouts again. Is it that man Sengi? Maryam's not sure. She hears the bang of the hatch as it's shut tight again. The roar of the sea disappears. Darkness returns. The women are talking. Their voices get louder as the boat rolls. Children wake up and cry. Maryam and her mother are thrown about by the boat's movement. In the dark, her mother's hand pulls her tightly to her as she sings a lullaby. It's the first time she's heard her mother's voice for hours.

'What's that?' A woman asks. 'I can feel water.'

'I'm sitting in water,' another says. 'It's up to my ankles.'

Maryam whispers to herself, 'Hooyo says stay small so the wind can carry me across the sea like a grain of sand.'

She feels a hand slipping into hers. It's dry. Rough. She recognises the long thin bony fingers.

An African woman sashays around the perimeter of the sun loungers, in tune with the gentle roll of the sea. Fabio watches her. The smooth movement of her hips keeps the pile of goods safe on her head; her hands hold out dangling necklaces and clusters of bracelets. He's thinking about what Marina said when she'd called after her dive. All the warning signs were there about the weather. She should never have gone. She should never have dived alone. At least she messaged him to say where she was. It's been tough since Albert's accident.

Hell, it's hot. Fabio knows he mustn't complain. It's his turn to look after the children. School holidays.

Marina's now at work. But he's still on call. That's how it is these days with the constant attention on the Mediterranean. It's been like this for some time. He checks on Lara and Stefano in the water. Bianco, the dog, runs up and down the rocks barking. Another hawker approaches Fabio, a small heavy sun-bleached backpack dragging at his shoulders. Fabio watches him weave around the sunbeds.

'Want box? Want box?' The man says in pavement English, standing between the sun and Fabio.

He takes off his backpack, pulls out a wooden box. Fabio glances at it and makes a small click of his tongue on the roof of his mouth. The box is tatty. He doesn't want it. But that's not the point. Everyone needs to earn a living. He asks the price and puts a grey blue five euro note in the man's outstretched hand. It closes like a clam.

Fabio's phone rings. It's Marina calling again. Something's wrong. He can hear it in her voice. She's talking quickly.

'A boat's gone down. Nanna just called me,' she says. 'They think it was early this morning. There were high winds last night. They think the boat came from Zawiya.'

Zawiya's a stone's throw across the Mediterranean, on the north Libyan coast. But still a perilous journey in bad weather. He thinks back to the conversation with Marina. All the signs were there. The wind, the sky, the colour of the sea. He pictures the heaving, rolling sea.

'The news said the boat was full of women and children,' Marina says. 'All locked in, down in the hold.'

Fabio must go to work. He knows he'll get a call any minute. He tells Marina he'll drop the children with Teresa, her grandmother. They'll need him at the Coast Guard office. He goes through the checklist of what happens when a trafficker's boat goes down on the Central Mediterranean route; all the different groups he will need to liaise with; the statistics he'll compile of those they find; estimates of those they don't; ID cards and papers that are always missing.

But where are the children? Fabio looks around him. He whistles for Bianco. Where the hell is the dog? He scans the beach, then the sea for Lara and Stefano. They're still in the water. Fabio waves at them. He shouts. He waves again. They see him and dive back under. His phone rings. It's Josef, his boss. He's been expecting his call.

'I won't be long,' Fabio says. 'I'm just dropping the children off and I'll be with you.'

He hears the sounds of the rescue services in the background.

'Fabio, we've found a body,' Josef says.

'A body? Already?' Fabio says. 'Well, that's a start. Hopefully, we'll find someone alive and then we can start the process of identification.'

'I'm not calling about the trafficker's boat,' Josef says.

Fabio scans the surface of the sea.

'We think we've finally found Albert, Marina's grandfather. One of the lampuki fishermen picked up a body earlier this morning, tangled in a net. We think Albert must have blacked out in the water,' Josef says. 'He still had his knife on him. At least, the currents

49

didn't take him and we have his body now.'

Fabio searches for the children. He's been distracted by the call. He thinks about Albert. He's relieved, in some ways. The uncertainty is over, the hope gone. But they can grieve properly. With a body it will help.

'Will you tell Marina and Teresa?' Josef says. 'Better coming from you.'

'Yes. I'll come into the office right now and speak with the team first,' Fabio says.

He hangs up. He hears a voice calling him. Papa! He turns. It's Lara, waving at him from the water. Where's Stefano? He can see splashing. He's under the water. All of a sudden, Fabio feels jumpy. It's the anticipation after a boat goes down. And now the news about Albert.

'Ejjew, ilkom biżżejjed fil-baħar u sar il-ħin,' Fabio shouts. Hey! It's time to get out of the water. 'Come now! Quickly. We're going.'

The Mediterranean gleams in the August afternoon, its surface flat like a sheet of glass over the seagrass beds. The cicadas vibrate. It's the hottest part of the day.

Ultramarine

Day two of the holiday. And Susan would like to say her view of the Indian Ocean is perfect. But she can't. From her sun lounger on the beach, she's already spotted a pesky plastic water bottle. It's bobbing on the surface of the sea in front of her, only metres from the shoreline, a morning arrival on the beach like herself. Susan's struggling to get into the holiday mood. It wasn't her idea to splash out and come all the way to East Africa. It was John's. He thought it would gee her up. She hasn't been herself for some time.

They agreed to go somewhere completely different from France, their usual destination. John said it would be good to have downtime together, to relax, for them both to enjoy themselves now that the school year had finished, reports were done, and Susan can stop working so ridiculously hard. But she loves her job. Loves her students, even the bolshy downright rude and difficult ones.

John came home one day and said he had found an

all-inclusive deal. And that was that. He said they needed to ring the changes. Date night seemed, well, that was why they were married, so they didn't have to do that. They'd briefly discussed home improvements like a new kitchen. But Susan's not much of a cook. And no, she didn't want an American-style fridge. In any case, there's only the two of them. Only the two of us, she says to herself, watching the plastic bottle as it moves along in front of her. And that's the problem. In a nutshell.

On her sun lounger, Susan leans a little forward to examine the ruler-straight horizon. How many miles away is it? The square root of what, multiplied by the… She leans back. Her mind goes woozy at the effort of trying to remember what John says on every beach holiday, about every horizon. It's a Pavlovian response. Spot the horizon. Measure it. What on earth is the point of measuring a false optical illusion? She knows what's on her horizon. Retirement! A terrifying thought. Not to have her work, her students, somewhere to channel her passion for all things artful and artistic. What on earth is she going to do? And John at home. Just the two of us. She knows she's repeating herself.

As an Art teacher, Susan can talk till the proverbial cows come home about her subject, if anyone cares to listen. By the end of term, her students were eating out of her hand. And not just her favourites. Yes, she has favourites and if any teacher says they don't, well they're frankly lying. Hamza, Mehdi and Bethany. There, she says it. As for her winning topic as a closure to the course, it was a triumph this year. She decided to do it on the colour blue. *Just* blue was not a colour. That was lazy, a cop out. Pants, she said, and the class had laughed at her use of slang. She goes through the whole talk in her head as she gazes at the Indian Ocean. But she stops mid-sentence, distracted.

Now, what colour is the Indian Ocean? It isn't cerulean although she adores the poetry of the word; azure has been ruined by the travel industry using it to describe every blinking stretch of sea other than the North Sea; cyan and sapphire—no, too dark and too cold. She decides the Indian Ocean in front of her is the colour, ultramarine, the word derived from the Latin *ultramarinus*, which means 'beyond the sea'. One thing Susan knows she's good at, is reading a room full of yawning students. And ignoring it. She does the one two boxing combination. One fact followed quickly by another fact—which has to be a knockout.

Once upon a time, she told them, the blue pigment was almost priceless, produced from lapis lazuli, travelling on the backs of donkeys, from a tiny corner of Afghanistan to Venice. Yes, Afghanistan! No, she told them, she wasn't going to talk about years of senseless unwinnable wars. She's talking about where lapis lazuli was found, the only colour deemed holy enough to paint the Virgin Mary's cloak. Who Miss? They jokingly said. The most painted woman in the history of the world, she had replied. Not photographed, not Snapchatted, not Tik Tok'd, not Insta'd. Painted! And respected and venerated. Susan's smiling as she remembers her final teaching session.

Now Susan feels a bit more ready for the day. Except she sees her phone lying beside her, earphones already inserted. She remembers. She'd made a pact with herself to finish the podcast, made by a famous couples therapist who promised help with any marital problem. Not solve, Susan noted. More's the pity. In the building heat, she closes her eyes. It would only be for a minute or two, she tells herself. John will be here soon. But if she doesn't finish the podcast soon, knowing John, he would grab her earphones and say, anything interesting? And start to listen. Maybe that wouldn't be a bad idea. One way of bringing the subject up. She'd better get on with it. Susan opens her eyes, then shuts them again immediately.

Instead of the Indian Ocean in front of her, she sees a woman. A vision of flawless human perfection. A woman, who just has to be French. Susan has watched enough French women on their summer holidays and in films to be confident in her assessment. It's all in the saunter, her slim hips and lack of inhibition. Perfect. Just perfect. Even the teeny, weeny bikini. And the colour. Saffron! Yes, saffron. Yellow with a hint of orange. Susan knows she would look like a reheated custard tart if she wore that colour.

Under the shade of her umbrella, Susan's self-conscious of how she's sitting on her sun lounger. She's in an Anglo-Saxon slump, listing to the right, like a sack of potatoes against a wall. Embarrassing. Unfeminine. Unchic. Un-French. In other words, just very English with a French goddess who's the polar opposite of her. She straightens herself and watches as the woman stands, brushing sea water from her shoulder length hair. The image of a long-stemmed Van Gogh sunflower in the heat of summer flashes through Susan's head.

The French woman bends and searches through her beach bag. She pulls out a packet of cigarettes. She uses her mouth to extract one. Susan hears the flick of a lighter. She's desperate for a cigarette. She gave up smoking years ago. It had become impossible to find anywhere to smoke in the whole of the United Kingdom where you wouldn't get wet, frozen to death or showered with looks of disapproval. And vaping's just not the same.

Beside the French goddess, Susan sees a man. The woman's husband? No, she has second thoughts. He seems too attentive. He's also lean, trim, tanned, with a shorn head of silver hair, and a gold chain around his neck. Utterly perfect as well. Just French sums them both up. The couple remind her of Serge Gainsbourg and Brigitte Bardot. She decides to name them after those French icons. A bit of fantasy is just what she needs.

Lying under her umbrella, Susan knows there's nothing she can do about the shade of her skin. She sighs at her zinc-coated body parts. She watches as Serge takes a squirt of oil from a small bottle. The smell of coconut mingles with the smell of cigarettes. He rubs the oil into Brigitte's back. Susan can't remember the last time John rubbed Factor 50 on her. He might have dabbed a bit on her nose or offered it to her like a tube of toothpaste, squeezing a smidge out for her to take.

She watches Serge's hand as it sweeps over and around Brigitte's hips, along her thighs, to her inner thighs and up to her... Susan pauses, trying to remember her school French. Yes. She has it. She remembers and says the word quietly to herself. Décolletage. She exaggerates each of the syllables, remembering the pronunciation of the acute accent over the letter 'e'. The French language, she decides, is like Brigitte's body. Full of angles and sharp corners. She, on the other hand, is full of soft corners and undulating contours. Susan sighs again. This looks like a prelude to sex. She imagines they'll soon go inside to their hotel room. She can't remember the last time she and John had sex. It just stopped without either of them noticing. It wasn't something she'd consciously decided on. Like going on a diet. Has John even noticed? They've never talked about it.

Susan glances at her phone again. That podcast! She's only got as far as the first episode. What was the title? You have to be honest with your partner. But first of all you have to be honest with yourself. No, Susan says to herself. She isn't in the mood for honesty. At least, she's being honest now. She puts her phone in her bag and takes out her book. She opens it. No, she says again, reading isn't what she wants to do either. Susan closes her eyes again and tunes into the soundscapes of the beach. As she lies quietly, she hears the shutters of the beach bar opening. That will be Samuel setting up for the day. Even with her eyes closed, she can tell there are more arrivals. She hears the high-pitched squeals of excited children, sandals on the boardwalk, ready to run onto the sand and into the sea with their lilos blown up, tucked under their arms. And, in the background, she hears the Indian Ocean quietly rushing in and lapping the beach.

A voice interrupts the hypnotic sound of the sea. 'Jambo, madam. How's your morning going?'

It's John. She'd left him at the breakfast buffet, plate in hand piled sky-high with food. High metabolic rate. Always hungry. She isn't much of a breakfast eater. Slow metabolic rate. He rolls out his beach towel on the sun lounger beside Susan and plonks his magazine and newspaper down. Susan knows it's only a pretence. He'll never actually lie down. There's always too much to do on holiday. She makes a silent bet as to what he'll say next.

'Well, jambo to you too. That's a hell of a start to the day,' John says. 'You should have messaged me. What on earth is she nearly wearing? And what a colour. I call that eggy yellow.'

Bet won. John has spotted Brigitte. Well, she's hard to miss. Susan can feel her holiday mood is in danger of ebbing further away if she isn't careful. Eggy yellow? It isn't John's fault. It's Brigitte's, inadvertently tapping into every unconscious and conscious negative feeling Susan has about herself. She opens her book again as a hint to John she's not going to start a conversation. Too early in the day. A puff of wind sends her bookmark scuttling along the sand. John puts his binoculars back to his eyes and watches it go.

'I've got it,' John says. 'I'll give you its coordinates when it settles. Fancy a mint?'

Susan watches John pull out a tube of mints from his shirt pocket.

'Spearmint Extra?' he says.

She shakes her head. The taste of coffee is still in her mouth: a nasty combination, mint and caffeine. John takes a mint for himself. She hears the mint rattling against the enamel of his teeth as he sweeps the shoreline with his binoculars.

'John,' Susan says. 'You're now standing right in front of me. And you're blocking my view. Shove over, for goodness' sake.'

'Thought you'd like to know, Samuel's got your bookmark,' John says, as he shifts his position away from Susan. 'He's down by the beach bar. He's just waved back at us to say he's got it. It's now in his pocket. Well, go on then. Give me an update on the action so far this morning. Reckon those two are French, don't you? Doing what we're doing. Avoiding a holiday in Europe with what's going on.'

He turns to hold up his newspaper. Susan reads the headlines. Too depressing. All over Europe. Heat waves. Fires. Political unrest. Terrorist attacks.

'Now, don't get lulled into a false sense of security about those two love birds. You know what the French can be like. Bolshy. Always on strike. And…' John pauses, 'Jean Cocteau was right.'

Susan looks at him. Has she really heard him say Jean Cocteau? Since when does John know anything about the French artist? And then she works it out. He must've been listening on the plane when she was talking about French surrealism, a topic she was going to research for a module next term. He was paying attention.

'Jean Cocteau says that the French are Italian people in a bad mood,' John says.

Susan laughs. She does find that funny. She can see John's pleased about that. They both love France. They really do. Apart from this summer, they always go to France on holiday. She absolutely loves how the French do things differently. She adores how dogs in France sit on chairs in restaurants, at tables covered with beautifully ironed white linen cloths. The bigger the dogs, the better. The more expensive the restaurant, the more dogs. She glances at John. He's now sitting on the edge of his sun lounger, reading his magazine. There's no one else she knows who asks for an annual subscription at Christmas to *Janes Defence Weekly* and reads it cover to cover, keeping himself briefed on all things military. Most men she knows ask for aftershave or soap on a rope.

'John, the French, they're not…' Susan says.

'Bolshy,' John says.

Susan sighs. I wish you would stop finishing my sentences. She looks across at the French couple. She wonders if Serge does that to Brigitte. She looks at John. Going on holiday, it's always the same. John packs binoculars; Susan packs teabags. John also packs a torch in case of power cuts and his Swiss Army penknife.

'Look! Uninvited guests entering the swimming area,' John says, looking up from his magazine.

Susan knew he wouldn't read for long. Ants in his pants already.

'We have a jet skier circling the swimming area where the children are. And now a white gin palace fast approaching the beach. They better keep well away from the kiddiwinkles, or I'll have to have words,' John says.

He isn't joking. Always a stickler for the rule book at all times, no matter where, what country and what continent. John looks through his binoculars.

'John, stop stalking that French couple.'

'Don't be silly. I'm looking at the boat about to anchor outside the swimming area. And the jet skier.'

Susan closes her eyes and visualises the scene in the water instead. John's commentary will be detailed enough. He chuckles away to himself.

'You're not going to believe this, Susan. But the boat's called *Just for Play*. That's worthy of a mention in our postcard home. Best be careful where you put the emphasis on that one, then.'

One thing she's always liked about John is his sense of humour. She hears the mint still swivelling in his mouth. It means he's deep in thought. Honestly, she can write a book on him.

'Tell me this. Why would you ride a jet ski, have the entire Indian Ocean to blast up and down on, and then decide to head towards a swimming area that's clearly demarcated for the littlies? Bloody bolshy, that's what I call it.'

Susan agrees. It doesn't make sense. But she's not that interested. She listens to the squeals and shouts. She imagines the children, their bottoms wiggling in the air like ducks diving for algae under the water.

'Oh well. I'll give them a few minutes before I march down and have words in my well-honed Swahili,' he says, putting his binoculars down on his lap.

Susan's pining for silence. With her book open again, she hopes John might take the hint. But she doesn't get past the first paragraph when she hears him suck his breath in over his teeth.

'What do we have here then? Beach Olympics coming up, I reckon.'

Serge is now standing in front of them, stretching his body. He takes his ankles in turn and stretches his quads, then his hamstrings and does a few side bends. He picks up a couple of bats and a ball.

'S'pose it's all right if you like a bit of French sausage,' John says.

Susan examines the fit looking Serge and wonders if he's a woodpecker in bed like John. She's sure he isn't. I'd quite like to go to bed with someone like that for a change, she says to herself.

'What do you reckon? Age wise? Fag end of fifty?' John asks.

'Who? Who are you talking about now?' Susan says.

'Keep up. I'm talking about the French What's-his-face. Do you reckon he's my age or older?'

Susan doesn't reply. It's obvious who's older. It's odd for John to make a comment like that, comparing himself to another man. Even though it's exactly what she was doing only an hour ago. Comparing every part of her with Brigitte. John scans the beach, turning his head to take in the full extent of the view from their sun loungers. He stops and lingers at the activity at the far end.

'Samuel's working flat out. Look at all those sun umbrellas arriving at the beach club now.'

Susan can just about make out a small group of workmen in luminous green overalls walking slowly down from the main reception of the hotel to the towel kiosk. But they're too far away. She'll have to put her glasses on if she's interested. But she isn't.

'Quick. Samuel's heading our way. Let's get ourselves a couple of drinks,' John says.

He calls out and waves at Samuel, who's walking briskly down the boardwalk path towards them.

'Jambo, Samuel. Looks like you're being kept busy,' John says. 'All those new sun umbrellas arriving.'

Samuel smiles. 'Jambo, jambo. I know. They're a surprise for me too.' he says. 'What can I get you today?'

'Well, you might want to have a word with that jet skier first,' John says. 'It's hovering outside the swim area. Looks like it might be trying to enter.'

Susan notices that Samuel isn't paying attention to John. He's looking back towards the far end of the beach, in the direction of the work men with the sun umbrellas still on their shoulders. She sees him frown.

'Give me a second please. I'll be right back. I need to check something out,' Samuel says.

He walks off quickly to the beach bar. John follows Samuel with his binoculars.

'Come on, John. Now you're stalking Samuel. Turn around and look at the game of beach tennis in front of us. They haven't missed a shot. And there isn't a wobble in sight. Must have asbestos feet in this heat. I can't even put my feet down on the sand.'

She counts aloud in French as the beach game continues. Quatre-vingt-deux, quatre-vingt-trois. She soon gets tongue tied. Despite their frequent holidays in France, her school-girl French has never improved. It's always the same number that trips her up. Eighty-four.

'That's odd,' John says, getting up from his sun lounger.

'What?'

'Something's not quite right. You know Samuel said he had to go and check something out. Well, he half ran to the beach bar, to talk to the workmen. Then I saw one of them shoving Samuel in the chest.'

'Shoving Samuel?' Susan says. 'Are you sure? It might have been one of those bro hugs?'

'No. It's quite an argument brewing. It's beginning to cause a bit of a stir.'

Susan hears the mint clicking against John's teeth.

'Fancy a walk, love?' John says, getting up and extending a hand to Susan.

'A walk? Now you're being ridiculous, John. You know how I hate exercise. Especially on holiday.'

'I've got a bad feeling.'

'Oh, that'll just be the change of food and water,' Susan says.

'It's not that, love. I think we should go for a walk. Right now. Something's not quite right. I can see Samuel's very upset. The arguing's still going on.'

'Oh, just ignore it, John. It's the busyness of summer with the arrival of new guests. They'll calm down in a minute,' Susan says. 'I'm sure it's not a serious row. Just heat and testosterone.'

'No, Susan. We need to get up and move. Now, Susan!'

Susan notices a rare tone in John's voice now. John, a man who is never serious unless absolutely necessary. It's also the repeated use of her name. He's talking quickly. He grabs her and pulls her up. A little roughly, Susan thinks. He keeps looking back down the beach in Samuel's direction with his binoculars.

'Let's go now! Do you hear? Just come with me. We need to move fast!'

Susan hears what she at first thinks is a single firework. She looks up at the sky. How silly. What on earth would she see on this brilliantly hot and sunny day against the blue of the sky? There was nothing in the hotel bulletin about fireworks. It would have said. She sees a white vapour trail from an aeroplane. She hears the sound again. John yells at the French couple. The small white ball drops onto the sand. Serge and Brigitte turn and look at him. They exchange glances and shrug. Serge picks up the ball.

'They're not getting it. I don't know what else to do,' John says.

The sound reminds Susan of their holiday last year in France and the Bastille Day celebrations. She remembers the loud bangs, crackles, whistles and hums in the warm balmy summer air of a French July evening. But there wasn't screaming at the Bastille Day fireworks last year. Susan is sure of that. Just happy cheering and shouting at the sight of the fireworks exploding in the velvet blue of a summer evening sky. She knows the difference between happy screaming and this, as John tugs her.

'We've only got fifteen seconds. We need to run in the opposite direction to the beach bar!'

John starts to shout at anyone and everyone.

'Run!'

He's sweating and breathing deeply.

'Run!' He shouts again.

'And don't look back, Susan. Do not look back. We need to be as far as possible from those people.'

'What people?' Susan says.

'The workmen carrying the sun umbrellas,' John says. 'I saw them. I saw them through my binoculars…' He catches his breath. 'I saw them put down the beach umbrellas in a stack. I saw them arguing with Samuel. And take out…'

Susan hears what John says next. Time slows to a second-by-second tempo. It's Susan's turn to tug at John. They both run. It's like an obstacle course as they zigzag through rows of sun loungers, large, opened umbrellas, children's sand toys and scattered flip flops and sandals. They run straight over carefully lain down towels. Susan tries to ignore the searing heat on the soft skin of her feet, the grains of sand rubbing in between her toes, the sharp pieces of bleached coral and shell. John repeats what he says to make sure Susan has heard him. Guns. He says that twice as they run. Guns concealed inside the umbrellas. And the jet skier has one too.

Up ahead, it's a smeary vision. Sweat drips down

Susan's face. Her sun cream stings her eyes. It's impossible to run on the sand. Her ankles roll. She falls to her knees. John pulls her up. Fifteen seconds is all they have. John's counting. And Susan counts too. No, it's less now. She realises they've lost time.

Ten, nine, eight.

In the distance, Susan sees people at the next hotel along from them on the beach. They're standing beside their coconut-fringed sun umbrellas, shielding their eyes with their hands, under the bright and full sunlight of the midday sun. They're looking straight at them.

Seven, six.

They point at Susan and John with outstretched arms. They wave. They call out. They whistle. They film, holding their mobile phones out in front.

Five, four.

'What on earth are they saying to us, John?'

'Keep running, Susan. Just keep running.'

Three. Two.

Susan runs until a woman grabs her, dragging her to a standstill. She sits Susan down and wraps her in a towel. Susan watches the security services sprint past on the beach, dressed in khaki from head to toe. They're holding rifles and wearing hefty handguns in holders strapped around their thighs. Not very camouflaged. She knows that's a ridiculous thing to think given the circumstances. She hears the noise of continuous firing and sirens. She turns slightly, glancing over her shoulder. Susan watches the rapid response teams shoot the gunmen dead. And then she faints.

In their hotel bedroom, the next day, John keeps repeating the same word. Surreal. He says it so often Susan tells him to shut up. It's getting on her nerves. He's getting on her nerves. It can't be surreal. It has happened. It has really happened. It is reality. It is fact. Not a fantasy in a piece of 20th century avant-garde art.

John changes the subject. He has a suggestion. He knows how Susan might be able to help. They all might find some small comfort if they can help. But Susan shakes her head.

'I can't.'

'Yes, you can. You might be able to give the police information,' he says, gently. 'You were on the beach long before me. You seemed very keen on the French couple.'

Susan shakes her head again. It isn't that she doesn't want to help. She's just reeling, reliving every moment of yesterday morning, every detail, even the colour of Brigitte's nail polish on her toes. Magenta. She remembers all that. And she can pinpoint exactly the moment her holiday went from people watching bliss to living nightmare. It was when Serge and Brigitte were on the cusp of one hundred with their beach tennis. They said it in French, of course. Cent! Triumphantly. And then John had shouted at her, that they had to run.

John's still talking. She knows it's his way of dealing with it. Her way is to stay quiet, bottled up. He says something about being lucky he's a keen reader of *Janes Defence Weekly* magazine. Lucky that his regular reading has kept him up to date on the trade in AK47s, the movement of weapons through Europe and overseas after the Balkan war. Cheap as chips.

'Lucky? Cheap as chips?' Susan shouts across the bedroom. 'People killed by guns that were cheap as chips?'

There's nothing John can say back to her. He shouldn't have used that trivialising expression even though it's true. Well, almost true.

'When I was a child, I just used to be frightened of crossing the road. Oh, and getting bitten by horseflies in summer,' Susan says.

Although John told her not to look back, she had. She saw the holiday makers behind her, near the beach bar. Dead. She saw the maimed, the children, their riderless lilos bobbing in the protected swim area. She had tried to spot Brigitte and Serge. But she couldn't. Susan keeps going over and over the shocking turn of events when they were idly watching the French couple playing bat and ball. She also marvels at John's presence of mind. How could he have been like that? So alert. She was all caught up in people watching. Fluff and trivia. John kept saying something. What was it? Ah yes. He kept saying they only had fifteen seconds. Why fifteen seconds? It was typical of John to be so precise and exact. It was like his obsession with measuring the horizon.

'John, how did you know we only had fifteen seconds?' Susan says.

John hesitates.

'Lucky I read *Janes Defence Weekly*,' he says again, making an apologetic face. 'I quickly calculated how far away we were, how fast the gunmen were moving with the typical firing range of an AK47. I came up with fifteen seconds. That's all we had. A guess, really. Nothing more than that.'

Susan walks across the room. John turns back to his laptop. He's checking the news on the internet. She stands beside him, putting her hand on his shoulder as she reads what's on the screen. John scrolls down, quickly skipping over the video of them running on the beach. It's already gone viral. He knows she won't like that. But Susan doesn't want to read the news report. She's searching for the posted photographs of the victims. She spots Serge and Brigitte, then Samuel.

'Stop, John. Let me read about them.'

Apparently, Serge and Brigitte weren't married. She was right. Both from Lyon. Brigitte was an office manager and Serge something in IT. And Samuel, he lived with his young family in the local village. Susan decides that she'll speak with the police. She wants to pass on messages to their families. She glances at the blacked-out bedroom window. She thinks back to the morning when she was lying on the beach. She looks at John who has just saved her life. Who has saved other people's lives on the beach as well.

'John,' Susan says.

John's still scrolling through the news on his laptop.

'John,' she says again more loudly.

He turns to look at her.

'I need to talk to you,' Susan says. 'We need to talk.'

Dear Mr President

Nico knows last night was different. In a run-of-the-mill execution nightmare, he's trying to escape from something or someone. But, this time, he opened his mouth to shout for help and nothing came out.

He pours milk into his morning tea. He'd gone to bed on edge after rowing with Sakura. The line was crackly. She didn't say where she was calling from. Nico tried to explain. She kept interrupting. Let me speak, he'd told her. I'm your father. I know the dangers, the risks faced by doctors on the frontline. I was a photojournalist, for Christ's sake! Women are not off limits. Sakura had called him a hypocrite before hanging up. That hurt. He takes a sip of his tea. That really hurts.

There were hostages in orange jumpsuits and gun-toting guards. Then the masks came off revealing toothy grins. Everyone was laughing. Surprise! Happy Halloween, Nico! Happy Halloween! Nico notices his hands shaking. He puts his mug on the kitchen table.

He's still thinking about the nightmare. There was one hostage left who hadn't taken off his mask. Or her mask. Mustn't read too much into it, he tells himself. But it felt real. Too real. The hostage scene reminds him of his time in Iraq.

Nico listens to the early morning silence. June's been a strange month so far. Flaming June. Unseasonably high temperatures, the hottest on record for decades, messing up the end of spring and the beginning of summer. There hasn't been a quiet slide from one to the other. He wonders where Sakura is. She never said. It's irritating him. And worrying him. He goes to his computer. Chip off the old block. He can see that in her.

As Nico sits in front of the screen, Sakura's words ring loud: *You were never there when we needed you. And now you think you have the right to tell me what to do.* Nico drinks the rest of his tea. His mind scans the globe, ticker taping through possible countries. He's never lost the knack and knowledge to divide the world quickly and cleanly into conflict and disaster zones. He hums and skips through the map in his head, like one huge snakes and ladders board of countries. Somalia, South Sudan, Iraq, Nigeria, Yemen, Pakistan, Syria. He moves on to the cities and territories within, with mythical, magical, even biblical names. He lingers over Yemen. He starts to type the word into the search bar. He tells himself it's impossible to know and ridiculous to even try to pinpoint where she might be going. Better not to know, he decides, and clicks out of the search engine. That's what he thought when he used to go off: impart knowledge on a need-to-know basis only.

That's exactly what Sakura's doing. Or, just baiting him with reminders of her childhood. It couldn't have been that bad.

Grabbing his camera from the kitchen table, Nico tells himself he's reading too much into the row. He goes out into the early morning. It's his ritual during high summer. The red valerian waves in the morning breeze. The nettles are high. He spots a nightingale. It follows him down the lane, nipping in and out of the hawthorn hedge. He listens for a song. Perhaps they've laid their eggs already. They're arriving earlier and earlier these days. He finds these individual acts of the natural order reassuring, like doing the washing up when someone's died. Like buying bread, come to think of it.

Nico walks towards the village shop, one hand steadying the camera around his neck. His knee hurts today. It must be because of the bad night. All that tossing and turning in pursuit of sleep. He thinks about the previous twelve months. He's been kidding himself that he was only visiting. Just passing through was how he explained his unexpected presence in the Kent village where his mother lived. She had left him the house, a house he'd put in moth balls. A house he thought he would never live in. No one was being nosey, just friendly and inviting him to drinks and nibbles, trying to place him and his dodgy knee. Like everyone else in his nomadic past.

Mister, where you from? He was always asked that question, mostly by children appearing out of nowhere and gaggling around him. Children in Iraq, in

Afghanistan, India, all fiddling with his camera, his lens, his lens cap, the buttons, his heavy camera bag. Stop it! he'd shout in whatever language or dialect was needed. Here, have a pencil! Stickers! And he would kick their ball down the street and pretend to barge them out the way. It was always the children he remembered and tried to forget. And that's what Sakura doesn't realise. He was always thinking of her, knowing she was safe growing up, far away from him and his work.

Now, Nico feels like a wounded King Salmon, limping back to a house he's never lived in, a photojournalist with a knackered knee, a broken marriage, a daughter who won't speak to him and a head full of nightmares. But, for the first time in a long time, he's feeling—and he hates to use that word—settled. His name appears on the utility bills, Nicholas Henderson. He's even painted the house name on the wheelie bins to placate his neighbour, Maureen. His footwear tells everyone who he votes for, what he eats and whether he recycles. He's a fully paid-up member of rural England. How humiliating. How depressing. It wasn't what he had dreamt of when he thought of coming home. But what did he dream of? He doesn't know. What he does know is what he'd said to Sakura on the phone last night. Been there, done that, got the t-shirt, Sakura. I know what I'm talking about. He shakes his head.

Nico sees Nobby waving at him through the shop window. That'll mean conversation. Just what I don't need. He pushes on the shop door and the bell announces his arrival. He steps carefully around Jessie who's lying on her front, lining up tins.

'We don't sell much tinned tuna these days,' Nobby says to Nico, catching his eye.

Nico gets it. He got it a while ago about the girl. He goes and picks up a newspaper. He can't help it. It's one of those engrained habits, checking in on what the old bosses are up to. He reads the front page and then thumbs through, looking for stories he's already read online. Oh, what's the point? It's all codswallop, fake news and malicious manipulation from gormless world governments to sandbag the truth. The post-fact world, what a mess. In my day, it was different. He shakes his head. That's exactly what he'd said to Sakura. In my day.

Nico hears snippets of Nobby's chit chat with another customer about doggie surgery. Poor sod had both removed. Christ, what the hell is that about?

'We still charge for those antiquated, soon to be obsolete newspapers,' Nobby says, turning towards Nico.

Nico puts the newspaper back.

'By the way, I've got a package for you.' Nobby disappears to the back of the shop.

Nico grabs a loaf of bread off the shelf, pulls out some loose change from his trouser pocket and counts the coins on the counter. He feels a tug on his camera strap. Jessie's now standing by him. She's the same height as his camera. He watches as she delicately squeezes the lens cover off the camera and removes it. She blows on the cover, then puts it back on with the same dexterity and precision she showed with the tinned tuna. She's seen me do this, Nico thinks. She's been watching me, spying when I've been out and about.

'Beautiful girl, my granddaughter, Jessie,' says Nobby, emerging with a package wrapped in brown paper, taped heavily at both ends. He puts it on the counter.

Nico immediately recognises the handwriting. It's from Sakura's mother. What now?

Nico and Nobby look at Jessie who's back on the floor.

'You're a favoured one this morning, Nico,' Nobby says. 'Normally prefers animals to people.'

Nico nods. He feels the same after all he's seen. He picks up the package and bread, turns to give Jessie a silent wave. He walks out the shop and heads home.

Hands full, Nico kicks open his front door. He drops the package and bread on the kitchen table. It's hot, stale and stuffy in the house. He takes out a knife from a drawer and slices open the package. Then he stops. It's a toss-up what's bothering him more. The heat or what his ex-wife might be wanting from him. He decides it's the heat in the house. He'll go through the package contents later. He checks all the downstairs windows, pushing them wide open, and heads upstairs, camera still around his neck.

At the bedroom window, Nico hesitates. There's a fleeting shadow out of the corner of his eye. He scans the garden. The magpies call out. Invisible and vocal. It's a warning cry. He sees the sleek flow of taupe, moving through the long blades of grass. With his naked eye, he takes in more than a camera lens can. His instinct is honed by years of looking first and pulling the trigger later. It isn't skill that bags the best photograph, he always says to people. It's patience.

The animal is in Maureen's garden now. It stops momentarily, standing on its hind legs. It sniffs the air and turns its head like a periscope, beady currant eyes alert, white throated. The magpies call out another warning. Nico positions himself so he can see the coop, camera in hand. He screws up his eyes to focus fully on the stoat. He hears the chickens. The chickens hear the magpies. Now the jackdaws join in. The chickens are trapped. He watches.

The stoat enters the coop, clambering up the wire fence. The chickens see it. They flap and try to flee. They squawk. They run. They half fly off the ground, airborne momentarily. Feathers scatter. Nico sees flashes of white with a whip of black from the tip of its tail as the stoat wraps itself around each victim, wrestling it to permanent flightlessness. The stoat rips each bird's throat out. It's quick, merciless and deft.

Nico has the whole sequence on film. He counts the feathered bodies. Eight. It didn't take long, he thinks. Roughly two a minute. A woman screams. It's piercing. For a second, he thinks the stoat has got Maureen. Victim number nine. The animal leaves the way it entered, cantering back up the fields. Job done. Not even a takeaway chicken in its jaws.

Nico runs down the stairs, out the back door and hops over the low partitioning fence. Maureen's standing in front of the coop, hands clasped to her face.

'Not again, Nico,' she screams. 'All gone. They're bantams. Smaller, easier to kill. Not one left alive. Pointless. Needless deaths.'

Pointless, needless deaths. The black curtain in his mind rustles. Pointless, needless deaths. Nico has seen a lot of them in his time. Too many. Somehow the camera he held between himself and the subject became like armour. Or so he liked to think, until he came home. And the nightmares started in all their technicolour glory. Like last night's. The panic attacks. The sweats. The irrational behaviour. Hard to hide at times.

Nico coaxes Maureen inside his house and makes her a cuppa. He promises to fix the coop for her. Make it killer proof, he says. He also knows he'll buy her more bantams to assuage his guilt as a voyeur, a spectator who stood by and did nothing. Not helpless. Just awestruck.

'But where's Jessie?' Maureen asks, looking up. 'She was supposed to come to collect the eggs.'

Next morning, Nico's in the dark room, his recently converted spare room. He's developed and dried the negatives. Now he's viewing them as the action with the stoat unfolds. It's savagely beautiful. No bullets, no bombs, no Semtex, no nails, just animal to animal survival. Or not, for the bantams. Better dying like that than as a battery hen, Nico decides. As he inspects each frame, he notices something in the corner. It's a small soft edge of a shadow he can't make out. He'll only know when he puts it in the enlarger. It's probably

Maureen. He can crop her out later.

Nico slides the negative strip into the carrier and centres the enlarger. He hears a sound. He ignores it. There's a slight irritation at the thought of being interrupted. Nico goes back to the negative. He wants to finish developing the film of the stoat. He hears more noise from downstairs. He stops. Stands rigid. Holds his breath. It's what he always did. It's second nature, this habit of listening, watching and waiting. 'It's nothing' is a phrase he hasn't ever subscribed to. A sound's a sound. He can feel his heart speed up. He breathes more deeply now. It's what Sakura has told him to do if he feels a panic attack coming on. In through his nose, out through his mouth. He does this for a minute. He breaks the sounds down. First he heard the turn of the cast iron latch. Then, the back door opened. The bottom of the door caught the edge of the mat. He heard the latch clunk back into place. But now, there's silence. It's gone quiet. He pauses and waits.

It's definitely a somebody. In the old days, there would have been an exchange of glances and signals. Wait. Stop. Listen. Okay. It's safe. Let's push on. But here, Nico's alone. He's standing in his darkroom. The safe light is on. He tells himself he's at home. In his own home. There isn't anything to take. His camera never leaves his side. The contents of his house aren't even worth cleaning, let alone stealing. He hears something fall, something small but compact. It's a dull thud on the lino.

He calls out.

'Hello!'

Silence. He waits again. He has an idea.

'Cup of tea?'

It's worked in the past to get him out of narrow squeaks and tight corners. It can't be Maureen. She wouldn't walk in without knocking. He hears a kitchen cupboard door open. Another thing he's been meaning to fix. It never shuts properly, the warped pine scraping along the frame. Never ignore the obvious. Rule of life. He pulls back the blackout curtain and walks slowly out of the darkroom. He goes down the stairs, one careful step after another, his knee throbbing. He steps into his kitchen. He's guessed right.

'Hello, Jessie,' Nico says.

The girl's lying on the floor by the sink surrounded by small tins.

'You're up early doors.'

Nico glances out of the window to see if anyone has come with her. He can't see anyone. She's come on her own.

'Just making myself a cuppa, Jessie. Fancy one?'

Nico puts the kettle on. Jessie has all the small-sized baked beans from the cupboard in one pile and is now working on the soups. Nico isn't used to company, let alone the company of a child. He wishes he had bought biscuits with the bread yesterday. When he turns, he sees the contents of the package sent by his ex-wife spread like a deck of cards on the kitchen table. Well, Goldilocks, Nico says to himself, who's been sitting in my chair? Suddenly, he goes cold and clammy. He knows these photographs. He thought he'd cleared everything from the house. Thought he had brought everything with him, the good, the bad and the ugly stuff. In his haste to leave, in the heat of the upheaval and yet another row, he must have forgotten these. He looks at the photographs fanned out in front of him. He doesn't need to see them. They're all indelibly printed in his mind, his psyche, in his body. It's what he's been trying to block out from his past.

Nico glances again at the photos in front of him. All of children. Boys in school uniform. Dusty. Scrawny. Brothers and cousins he'd been talking to on their way back from school. About Jessie's age. They're grinning at the camera, fooling around, showing off. Tongues out, V-signs, the peace one and the other, making faces. These were children who would have been at home if they hadn't had seen his camera and all his paraphernalia and lingered those extra minutes with him. When they'd realised how late they were, they ran off laughing. He heard their sandals loose and flapping under their feet. He turned and saw the backs of them as he went in the opposite direction. Just before the US military airstrike. Seconds. That's all it takes. Blown to smithereens. All that happened to him was a knackered knee.

That's what he wants to talk about with Sakura. How life can change in a moment. That's all he wanted to say to her the other night, if only she had let him speak. And to tell her about her name, a reminder, a reminder to him at least. Not because of its association with nature and the Japanese cherry blossom. Well, of course, that too. But it's more a reminder of how ephemeral life is. How living is a matter of luck. Jessie now has the tins in lines of four, straight as a ruler with millimetre perfect spacing. Nico quickly gathers up the photographs. Another life, he thinks, but definitely not another world. He puts them away.

Jessie stands and comes to the table. Grown-up stuff all this death, doom and destruction, Nico thinks. Well, it should be grown-up stuff. She picks up Nico's hand. She gives him a tug and leads Nico to the back door. It's a rare sign of trust, when a child like Jessie does that, choosing an adult to show them something. Nico knows that. He should go with Jessie. He can finish developing the negatives later. He just needs to have a cup of tea and collect himself. The photographs of the boys have rattled him. Jessie opens the back door. The phone, on the far kitchen counter, rings.

'Jessie, just wait a second, love. I need to answer this.'

For a moment, he thinks it might be Sakura. Nico feels another tug. Jessie still hasn't let go of his hand. He shakes her off. He doesn't mean to be so rough. He tries to move quickly to reach his phone. But the ringing stops. He's been too slow. His knee hurts. The caller has hung up. Nico looks at the screen. There's no caller ID. He tries voicemail. Nothing. It's probably a scam call. Happens all the time, he tells himself. Or about his smart electricity meter. Ridiculous to think Sakura would call after everything that was said.

Nico turns to speak to Jessie. But Jessie's gone. Disappeared. He looks around the kitchen. The tins are still there. The back door is wide open. He should have been paying attention to her. He was expecting a quiet day in the dark room. He's not used to anyone dropping in, let alone Jessie who's opened his post. And now she's run off God knows where. And it's all my fault, he thinks.

Grabbing his camera, he goes out the back door. He walks as quickly as he can. He needs to find Jessie. It's the rule of the village. All eyes on Jessie. He has an idea. The path at the back of the house is like an old roman road. Straight, lined with tall lilac wafting scabious flowers, a perfect path to wander down and see butterflies, dragonflies and bees. That's the first port of call. Nico knows it like the back of his hand. He's been photographing it for months. The tall grass is alive. Insects ricochet in and out of hedges, bursting with summer. Stinging nettles are shoulder high.

Nico waves his way through, limping. His eyes skim the middle distance up ahead. His mouth is dry. He tries to go faster. The camera bangs into him, tapping his breastbone. He's feeling like one of those bantams—headless, flightless, and panicky. He's responsible. Jessie has come to his house. That stupid phone call distracted him. Not paying attention. Always distracted by work. What did Sakura say? Never there when we needed you. Jessie just disappeared in a puff of smoke. In seconds. That's all it takes. That's all it ever takes. If he'd paid attention to Jessie, they would both still be at home in the kitchen having a cup of tea.

The black curtain in his mind rustles. It's been threatening all day. He's been trying to ignore the signs. The package contents are pushing him to an edge. Up ahead he sees something. He slows his pace. It's the top of Jessie's head. He breathes again, just how Sakura told him. He knows he mustn't call out. When Nico gets within striking distance of the girl, he raises his camera and takes photos. The shutter clicks loudly. Jessie lifts her head like a deer sensing danger. She sees Nico. Nico knows what to do. No surprises, no sudden movements, no physical contact, only explaining in a clear and confident tone what he's doing.

'Hello, Jessie,' Nico says. 'Just wondered if you wanted to take some photos with me. And come home for a slice of bread and jam?'

Nico's now alongside Jessie.

'Is it okay if I look?' Nico says and half squats beside her.

He winces at the pain in his knee. There's a dead frog on the path, its guts spewed out. So that's what Jessie found and wanted to show me, Nico thinks. He looks at the creature, its lungs, liver, stomach, intestines flattened into a single red flat-packed surface. He feels relief it's only a frog. He stands. He knows what's coming next. He can tell. It's not the heat. It's not the change in his position or blood pressure. The smallest associations can trigger him. It's the sound of his feet on the gravel path, his camera heavy on his chest, foot hold slipping on small stones, the dust kicking up, his dry mouth, panic, running flat out. And the children. All of them. Those boys. Every single one of them that he had met.

Jessie takes his hand. She tugs his arm. She points at something ahead. Nico follows where Jessie is pointing.

He watches as the coil moves in a single motion, revealing its black diamond zigzag down its creamy white back. It changes shape and form, evaporating into the hedge as if something or someone has pulled it gently through like a silken thread.

'It's an adder, basking on the warm gravel,' Nico says. 'Lucky us.'

He hears a small intake of breath beside him. Jessie has her hands in front of her face, her fingers creating a square. She takes a photo, making a click with her tongue on the roof of her mouth.

Nico's back in the dark room. He's prepared the test strip and the proof sheet. He has the enlarger set. The negative carrier is in place, the photographic paper in the easel. He whips out the paper from under the enlarger.

'Now. The magic show begins. Abracadabra,' he says.

It's an old love, developing film. He drops the paper into the developer tray, letting it sit, undulating. He nudges it, agitating the liquid so it swirls and washes around it. Within seconds, the black-and-white image appears. Nico flips the paper over, then flips it back again. He checks the timer. He counts the remaining seconds. Keeps an eye on the developer tray.

The bantams are emerging. It's a thrill, every time, to see an image reveal itself. It's magical. But he notices something in the corner of the image. Ah, the shadow. In the frame just before the action of the stoat killing the bantams in the coop, with feathers flying, with razor-sharp teeth snapping through necks, there is someone. He looks closely. It's not Maureen. The shadow's too small. He knows exactly who it is. Jessie, crouching on the grass outside the chicken coop. She was there. A ringside seat. She saw it all. All eight bantam deaths. She was definitely too late for egg collecting.

Nico's phone rings. Not another interruption. He stops a moment. He can't answer it. His phone is downstairs in the kitchen. He never brings it into the dark room because of the light. He'll finish what he's doing and check his voicemail later. The black-and-white image floats in the tray. In any case, if it's Sakura, he knows what he needs to do. He knows what he should have done, should have said, a long time ago.

Early evening, Nico listens to Sakura's message for the umpteenth time.

Dad, are you there?

'I am,' says Nico as he holds the phone to his ear.

Sakura says where she is. He was right. Yemen. He hears her pause. What did you use to say, Dad, when you came home? Not a lot. He rarely said anything about his work. She says she has to transit through London. She'll come by and see him in a month when her visa runs out. He hears the edge in her voice.

As Nico stands by the kitchen window, he glances at the letter sitting on the counter, waiting to be posted. Should have done that years ago, he thinks. As soon as I had left Iraq. Why didn't I? The row with Sakura has stirred him now, prodded the bear. It was also the shock of seeing the photograph of the Iraqi boys again. Nico thinks back to earlier in the day when he'd sat down with his laptop and typed into the search engine the U.S. President's name at that time. The ex-President's name. George W. Bush Jr. Up he popped and his address in Texas. He quickly found some paper. Yes. He wanted to write a letter by hand. At first, he wasn't sure what he was going to say. He wrote: *Dear Mr President* and paused. Then Nico couldn't hold back. He described how he had met the five boys, walking home after school. They'd stopped. Mister, where you from? They'd fooled about in front of the camera. Nico knows who was tallest, the youngest, the best at keepie-uppies. By now, they'd probably have their own families, he wrote. If they'd lived, he added. Pointless, needless deaths, he underlined. Nico wasn't a bystander; he was a witness. He enclosed the black and white photograph with the letter. He'll go see Nobby tomorrow for a stamp.

Nico thinks about autumn and acorns dropping in their green jackets; next spring and the robin nests filled with perfectly smooth pale-blue eggs, and then summer with the hard-to-spot Purple Emperor butterflies courting in the oak canopies and the whirligig beetles in pond water. Behind him, he hears the turn of the cast iron latch, the drag across the mat as the bottom of the door catches its edge. The latch gives its usual clunk as it goes back into place.

Slå katten af tønden

Amara can't stop thinking about the dead birds. They've been coming for months now. Even last week, as she was leaving Copenhagen for West Jutland, there'd been one on the doorstep of their house. The first dead bird had appeared back in the summer, shortly after opening her new café in Copenhagen. Then the second one came. The third was the most shocking. She'd found it inside the café by the oven in the kitchen. The social media trolling kicked off. It was all because she was interviewed on the television news and had let rip about the lack of job opportunities for children of immigrants.

Sitting cross legged in front of the large window of the West Jutland cottage, Amara faces the vast open heathland that runs into sand dunes, the lighthouse and the sea beyond. She squints at the steel-grey horizon. She can barely distinguish sea from sky from land. The freezing wind's coming off the North Sea, whipping up waves. The countryside's dark and flat. She hasn't seen her shadow for months: a Danish winter is long and dark. Up above, a skein of geese flies over, in a V formation, battling the wind. One of the geese at the front drops to the side. Amara watches as it falls away exhausted, spoiling the near-perfect aerial unity.

The geese remind her of the dead bird in the café kitchen. After she found it, Amara called 114. She'd called the police from the café with all the noise so that no one could hear her conversation, with taps running, plates clattering. The police said to keep it tight. Not to say much to anyone, including friends and family. Even Matthias, her boyfriend. She's been keeping it so tight, she feels like a fish gulping for air in a bucket. Which is why she shut the café early, at the peak of the run up to Christmas, and left. She had to get away.

'Jesper,' Amara says. 'So, what do I do now?'

Jesper's in the kitchen, at the counter. They're childhood friends, having bonded over who had the worst costume for Fastelavn and the school parade. Amara was also the girl with no friends. She stank, the other children said. It was her hair. It smelt of her mother's cooking. She'd begged her mother to stop cooking food that was different from everyone else's. In their teens, it all changed. This ugly duckling, all limbs and uncoordinated, became beautiful. Even Jesper told her that. He said she looked like the national bird of Denmark. The swan.

Jesper's come from Aarhus to be with her. To sit it out. They haven't seen each other for months. His hunting knife lies across her lap. She picks it up and runs the sleeve of her sweater over the leather handle, polishing it. She watches him make an incision around the neck of the dead rabbit he's holding. He peels the skin off the carcass.

'It's pretty clear to me, Amara,' Jesper says as he holds up the rabbit skin to show her. 'If you show fear, it means you accept you're prey.'

Amara makes a face. She knows what Jesper's really saying. He's telling her she needs to return to Copenhagen and open the café back up. In other words, show no fear. Get back to normal and face the music. Closing before Christmas was crazy. He'd already said that to her. No matter how scared you're feeling, don't let them win. They want you to close the café. They want you to go out of business.

'Anyway, tell me again what the police said to you?' he asks.

Amara thinks back to the conversation. It was with a woman. She spoke Danish like her mother. Slightly accented. A misplaced inflection here and there. That's what made Amara talk so much. She blurted out about the trolling, the dead birds, and how she didn't feel safe. And now there are footprints in the garden. Amara was asked about the house. Where she lived. How protected. Can she be seen from the road? Amara told her it was floor-to-ceiling glass. There was silence at the other end of the line. No curtains? Not even shutters? Amara shook her head. It was Matthias's dream house. As an architect, he designed it as a passive house. No need for anything like that.

'You know that tradition at Fastelavn, Amara? The one we all learnt about in school?' the police woman said. 'Slå katten af tønden.' Beat the cat out of the barrel.

Amara knew exactly what the policewoman was talking about. She remembered learning about the medieval tradition. It's no longer a real cat inside the barrel; it's more a piñata game now.

'Your situation is like that,' the policewoman had said. 'And, you're the cat, Amara. You're that cat in the barrel. Just go away for a while. I know it's nearly Christmas and it'll be difficult. But do it. And change your mobile number. Put a camera up on the front door and others around the house. You know, one of those fancy smart entry phones that notifies you when there's someone around.'

Amara thinks about the footprints in the garden. Because it's winter, she can see them clearly in the snow. It's obvious people know where she lives, where she and Matthias live. She did get the cameras installed. She switched on the entry phone the day she'd left for West Jutland. Amara looks at Jesper who's now cutting up the rabbit carcass. She decides to follow the police advice and not say much, to keep it tight.

'They said to just keep a low pro,' Amara says. 'You know, keep off the radar. Go offline.'

Matthias is at home. It's not long until Christmas. His parents are expecting him and Amara for dinner on the 24th. Juleaften, Christmas eve. Matthias has already told them that they're both coming even though Amara's still in West Jutland. She's been there a week now. He's worried about so many things. The café being closed. The suddenness. The financial hit. The damage to Amara's reputation as a serious businesswoman trying to break into the new Nordic food scene. The trolling. And now the footprints in the garden.

In the evenings, on his own, he's in the habit of playing the video message Amara made on the day she left Copenhagen for the cottage. She was standing right where he's now sitting. In their living room. He picks his phone up and taps the screen to start the video. Amara appears.

'Hi darling. It's me. I'm just about to leave. Everything is set at home. Let me give you a quick pan of the house. Hope you like it. I went all out with candles.'

Matthias looks at the candles, dotted around the downstairs of the house. He hasn't lit any of them, hoping she would be back by now so they could do it together. He stopped lighting the Christmas calendar candle the day Amara left for West Jutland.

'What else? You just need to wrap the presents for Lars and Birgitte. We'll take them on Christmas eve. Oh, and it's such a beautiful day. Have you had time to look out of the window? It's started to snow already! See the pine trees. They've already got snow along their branches.'

So, Matthias says to himself, Amara is saying she's coming back. There's nothing to worry about. He keeps telling himself that, even though the message is now a week old. Plenty of time for her to change her mind about Christmas if he really thinks about it. He doesn't want to. He tries not to. He turns his phone to landscape. He feels dizzy when Amara pans the room, making a joke with a close up of the Arne Jacobsen chair, his Arne Jacobsen chair, that he's sitting in right now. The camera jiggles. She'd decorated the house as a surprise for him. It looks so homey. So cosy. His home. Their home. Possibly. They weren't quite there yet.

That's what his parents think. Early days. Don't rush things, his mother, Birgitte, keeps on saying to him. She says it often. Too often. It's beginning to irritate him. Take your time, his father, Lars, said. He'd only said it once and then said, ever heard of the joke about the impetuous Dane? No? Well, that's because there isn't one. Nothing explicit is said. Well, nothing much. It's more his mother. Matthias knew what she meant when she'd said to him: Amara? That's a beautiful name. Where's that from? And he had replied, Aarhus. Matthias hopes his mother got his point about Denmark's second largest city. They've never discussed it since.

It's the next bit in the video that reassures Matthias when he's feeling unconfident about Amara and their future. It's the joke Amara makes towards the end of the video.

'Okay darling. I need to go. I'll be fine. Don't forget to feed the cat! Bye!'

The cat. That's their joke. It's a joke in lieu of discussing marriage and commitment. Commitment is having a cat together, so they both say. There were all sorts of reactions when he'd told friends and family he'd met someone else after he'd split up with Katrine. So soon! What? She asked you out? Amara wasn't who anyone was expecting. He wasn't expecting to meet her either. He thought he would have a break after Katrine. He met Amara at a dinner. She asked him if he likes sculpture. He found himself nodding, saying yes, and then thinking, oh, Christ, no, I don't. And she said, let's meet at the Thorvaldsens Museum. No one ever goes there. We'll have it all to ourselves. He did. And they did have it all to themselves.

Matthias watches the video until the end where Amara puts her coat on and jokes about the new entry phone. She said it would make it easier to see the Christmas elves. But there wasn't anything funny in that. They both know why she'd installed it. She's been cagey since she spoke to the police. He's trying not to read anything into that. They're both feeling the pressure of the situation. Matthias has also been following the threads and feeds on Facebook and Twitter. It turned nasty very quickly. It is nasty. The last post rammed it home to Matthias. He knows it could just be a crazy crackpot or a completely sane keyboard warrior who picks her kids up from the forest kindergarten and then makes cookies with them for the rest of the afternoon. Or some kind of stalker. Most likely a man. Though possibly it's a woman. He can't share any of this with his parents. They won't understand. They'll only want to follow the family tradition. Let's keep it all smooth, especially coming up to Christmas when all we want is to be cosy.

Matthias puts his phone down. He hears the front doorbell ringing. He's not expecting anyone. He's cautious. He looks at the camera view on the entry phone. Sees who it is. And opens the door.

'Pillows? You're kidding me,' Jesper says.

'You know what it's like when you stay at someone else's house, as a guest. You notice all these different things. Their pillows. They're not like ours. I don't sleep so well,' Amara says.

'So, what's for Christmas?' Jesper says. 'You know. From the in-laws?'

Amara gives him a dead arm.

'Not in-laws,' she says. 'Not yet.'

'It'll be one of those cream cable knitted sweaters, like in the TV ads they show about Denmark at Christmas. Happy matching families!' Jesper says.

Why does Jesper have to point out the differences between her and Matthias's family? Despite their whirlwind romance, she thinks she knows Matthias. But when she sees him with his parents, he vanishes in front of her eyes. They speak about memories, events she has never been part of. But she knows them off by heart now. Remember when we all rolled naked in the snow… and that time you gave me that chilli to eat and swore it wasn't hot… and when we camped and the mosquitoes ate us alive… let's not go back to that. Matthias and his parents all laugh at what each other says. All the time. They really laugh. They make silly noises together. They josh and jostle each other. It's beautiful. Amara can see that. Yet, at the same time, it's painful, the not being part of it, standing on the outside. It also feels like a tug of war. Push, pull. Amara doesn't want to fight. She can also see something in Birgitte's eyes. It's fear; fear of losing Matthias. To her.

'So, what does your mama think?' Jesper says. 'Has she even met Matthias?'

Amara hesitates, then shakes her head. Not yet. There hasn't been time, the right moment, what with the café and then her moving into Matthias's house. She's avoiding it. Saying very little about him except he wasn't like them. Her mother had gone silent. The only thing her mother had said was, will he learn our language? It had pulled her up short. Of course, he's not going to, Amara had said to herself. She's never told her mother that she no longer dreams in their language. She feels like a chameleon, morphing into Amara who has a life in the bright lights of Copenhagen, and then Amara who goes back to Aarhus, and the family flat, in the low rise.

'What are you waiting for?' Jesper says. 'Christmas?'

'Very funny,' says Amara.

But she's not in a hurry to go back to Copenhagen. At first, she thought she'd only be away for a few days. Now, a week's gone by. She's in touch with what's going on at the house because of the security cameras. She can see who's coming and going. Amal came on Tuesday to clean. Johannes the postman too. But then a notification came in from the smart entry phone last night. She'd played the security video. She saw the back of someone wearing a long coat. When Matthias had opened the front door, the person had slipped the hood off. Amara knew then who it was. She'd seen a photograph at Matthias's parents' home when they'd gone over for lunch one weekend in the early days. It was on the bookshelf in the living room. Didn't know you had a sister? she'd asked Matthias. The next time, the photograph had gone.

It was Katrine in the photograph and Katrine on her doorstep, their doorstep. She couldn't see Matthias because of the camera angle. They stood there for a moment talking before Katrine went into the house. Amara plays the video message one more time before she deletes it.

'I've decided, Jesper. I want to go home for Christmas,' she says. 'To Aarhus.'

Amara says she'll message her mother and tell her they're on their way. They can be there in a couple of hours. Her mother won't be expecting her. She thinks she'll be working flat-out in the café. She'll have to decide what to say to her mother. Her sudden arrival home will cause worry, closing before Christmas. Her mother always worries about money.

And then there's Matthias and his family, Amara says to herself. What am I going to say to him? To them?

It's December 24th. Matthias parks outside his parents' house. As he walks slowly up to the front door, he sees the kitchen window ajar. He stops. It's the familiar smells of Christmas. Aromas of flæskesteg, crispy pork, and roast duck with pickled red cabbage waft out of the kitchen into the freezing winter air. Through the main window he spots his father on the stairs. He watches him adjust the trail of Christmas decorations—the paper stars, the paper hearts—on the staircase. It's a typical Christmas scene between his parents. His mother in the kitchen, his father tweaking the decorations that must be in exactly the right place. He thinks back to the phone call he made only a few days ago, when he told his parents Amara had to change her plans and was now not coming for Christmas dinner. He didn't say much. Didn't explain beyond saying her brother had returned unexpectedly. He had to make up an excuse. There wasn't much else to say. He was confused. Speaking on the phone with Amara has been difficult. She hasn't been herself for a while. No one's been themselves.

There's been an elephant in the room ever since his parents saw Amara and her new Nordic café on the news. It's a touchy subject. Too touchy to talk to his parents about. It feels increasingly hard to keep walking around the elephant. There are so many things they all need to talk about. To clear up. Since the news report, the only thing Matthias has said was that social media had kicked off. But his parents hadn't asked about that. And he hadn't volunteered more information.

Through the window, Matthias watches his father pour a glass of gløgg. He can tell his parents are in the middle of a conversation. His mother's frowning. He's wondering what they're talking about. Who they're still talking about. There's a rub between Birgitte and Amara. His mother likes everything smooth and cosy. And Amara, well, she's got a different take on life. That's what he noticed the minute they met. What did she say when they had their first family dinner? Something like, oh I think in Denmark we try to be too like our Christmas biscuits. Vaniljekranse. All sweet and sugary. It's much better to think of life like the flat bread I make in the café. Sweet, spicy, bitter and salty. That's Amara. She doesn't dress things up.

Matthias opens the front door, letting in a gust of cold air. The curtains move, the flames of the lit candles shimmer. There's a flurry of snow on the shoulders of his coat. He stands in the front hallway and takes his coat off. His parents call out to him. He puts the presents he's brought by the tree. Matthias glances at the table. It's laid for four, even though he's already told them Amara won't be coming. The whole perfect picture of Christmas irritates him. It's as if his mother hasn't listened, that she's still trying to curate some Christmas magazine editorial to export to the rest of the world. He spots the napkins. They're folded into some intricate, snowflake kind of design.

'Let's sit down and have a drink,' Lars says, hugging Matthias.

His mother comes out of the kitchen and gives him a kiss. But Matthias is on edge. Before he left, he saw more footprints in the garden, ones he can't explain even though he tries to tell himself it's probably neighbours. Except they're old and their grandchildren don't play football in the snow. Despite sweeping away the snow, the footprints keep returning. Whoever it is, cleverly avoids the cameras on the house. He just doesn't know how. Yes, he does. It's because they're watching the house. His parents ask him about his work and the Christmas lunches. He tells them he's been busy, rushed off his feet. In fact, he's turned a few invitations down. He's been at home more than usual. Waiting.

They sit to eat. No one removes the place setting for Amara. Lars pours drinks as Birgitte brings out the food. Matthias puts his hand over his glass. He notices his mother and father glance at each other.

'Not staying the night, Matthias?' His mother says.

Matthias tells her he hasn't decided. His father is already quite tipsy. He's singing. Matthias joins in. They tell each other stories about their last sailing trip they made together at the end of the summer. His mother's smiling at them. They're laughing about when one of the ropes jammed at the bow. Matthias had to crawl carefully along to release it. The wind was strong. Matthias teases his father, did you deliberately let the boat keel over so far? His father laughs. Matthias feels himself relax a little. He's slipping back into the fold, the traditions and patterns of family. Of cosiness.

Birgitte gets up from the table. The main course plates are cleared. She heads to the kitchen. She tells them she won't be long. Just finishing off the risalamande, the rice pudding. But Matthias knows Birgitte has deliberately left him and Lars together. That's the usual tactic. Birgitte issues the brief and Lars executes. But his father will avoid tricky conversations, particularly on Christmas eve. When Birgitte comes, Matthias waits for his father to make a joke about the Christmas elves, out there in the woods in the dark. Lars loves the traditions and the old fairy tales with their dark stories. They're just like real life, he always says.

His mother serves the risalamande onto plates and passes them around. Matthias thinks about the whole blanched almond in the dessert. Last year, Katrine found it. He remembers that. They had had Christmas dinner with her family. All sitting around this table this time last year. Matthias watches as his father takes a spoonful and puts it in a bowl they always use for the elves.

'Now, we mustn't forget to feed the Christmas elves,' Lars says. 'Otherwise, there'll be trouble. You know what the elves are like playing their pranks and tricks all the time.'

His mother gets up and takes the bowl for the elves.

'We don't want any more trouble, do we?' Birgitte says as she walks away from the table.

Matthias puts his spoon back down. He's heard his mother loud and clear. He knows exactly what she's really saying. It must be the wine that has made her speak up like that. For months, Birgitte has swept every difficult conversation under the carpet. What she means is that Amara is causing trouble, too much trouble. That's just how his mother is. Never says things directly. He thinks back to Katrine's visit. She had come round to tell him about Birgitte. How Birgitte keeps calling her to have coffee, a walk, lunch even.

'You're right,' Matthias says, 'we don't want any more trouble.'

There's an immediate silence. Matthias has heard the edge in his voice. Birgitte turns and comes back to the table. She puts the bowl down. She sits.

'What do you mean?' His father says.

'You know exactly what I mean. It's all got to stop right now,' Matthias says.

His parents exchange glances. Matthias turns to his mother.

'I know what's going on. You're the one causing trouble. You must stop calling Katrine.'

Matthias spots the surprise on his father's face, obviously unaware of Birgitte's phone calls.

'Katrine doesn't want to have coffee with you. It's awkward for her. She came round the other night to tell me,' Matthias says. He knows there's one more thing he needs to say. It's time to get to the elephant in the room. 'It's not Katrine and I anymore. It's over. And stop making Amara feel like an uninvited guest.'

He looks at his mother's flushed face. His father tries to get his attention. Some fatherly advice is coming across the Christmas table. Keep it smooth, son. Too late! But there's also something else bothering Matthias. What he doesn't say to his parents is that ever since Katrine came round, Amara has hardly called. The last time was to tell him that she was going back to Aarhus for Christmas. Made some kind of excuse about her brother coming home unexpectedly.

Matthias picks up his spoon. He feels something round and hard as he puts a small amount of rice pudding on his spoon. Ah, he says to himself, I'm the lucky one this year. His mother probably made that happen. He works his spoon around to avoid the almond. He doesn't want it. He wants to leave. Jump in the car and drive to Aarhus. He's been thinking about doing that all day. The roads will be quiet. But he keeps hesitating. Amara hasn't invited him. And there's always the prospect of Jesper. He knows Jesper has been keeping her company at the cottage in West Jutland. Despite how many times Amara has told him they're only friends, he's never entirely sure. If he surprises Amara, would Jesper be there too? There's always this cliquiness, a closeness, a history that he and Amara don't have.

Matthias puts his spoon back down. He folds his napkin slowly and puts it on the table. His parents watch him. He pushes his chair back and stands. He goes round to where his mother is sitting across the table and kisses her. Then his father.

'I need to go,' he says. 'I'm sorry. I think I left a candle burning at home.'

His parents glance at each other again.

'Will we see you tomorrow?' Birgitte says. 'Will you join us at church?'

As he drives home, Matthias wonders how life can be the best and the worst with Amara.

In Aarhus, that same night, Amara and her mother are in the kitchen. They're packing up food from dinner.

'But you're going back to Copenhagen, aren't you?' her mother says. 'Soon?'

'I've only just arrived!' Amara says. 'Why are you asking?'

'Well, Jesper....' her mother says. 'Jesper said something about... Anyway, your café. I expect there's lots to do as you've only opened it this year. You know, to make it a success. Pay off the loan you took. That's the most important thing.'

'But Jesper said what?' Amara says.

'He said something about you being in trouble,' her mother says. 'And I'm worrying about money, money you might be losing with the café being closed whilst you've been here.'

'It's only been a few days.'

But her mother is right about the financial impact. And, it's been more than a few days since she closed the café. She hasn't told her mother about being in the cottage in West Jutland. There's a lot she hasn't told her mother. But what has Jesper said? She thought they'd agreed to say nothing about the backlash after the television interview.

Her mother's putting the lids on the food containers.

'There's always something, Amara. Trouble seems to find you. Speaking your mind. Putting your head above the parapet.'

Glædelig jul, happy Christmas, Mama, Amara says to herself. Now it's all coming out. She thinks back to the conversation with the police woman. Slå katten af tønden. It's exhausting. It's frightening. She doesn't know what to do. If she told her mother what's really going on, she knows the advice her mother would give her. Just avoid trouble. Amara takes the food containers across to the fridge.

'And Matthias…' her mother says.

'You can't say anything yet. You haven't met him,' Amara says, turning her back to her mother. She knows her mother wants to say something more about Matthias. She knows what her mother wants to say. She closes the fridge door. She's glad her brother isn't here. He would probably side with their mother.

'Mama, I'm not like you,' Amara says. 'You know, fitting in. It's never been my way. I'm not like that. Even if…'

She hears her phone ring. She's not sure what she was going to say. It would only worry her mother if she told her about the dead birds, the footprints in the garden, the trolling. Amara walks quickly to the living room to find her phone. She's missed the call. It's Matthias. Of course, it's Matthias. They haven't spoken today. Both avoiding a conversation. She notices the video message he sent earlier. She's delayed watching it until now. She sits on the sofa and presses play. The video starts.

Matthias is sitting in his chair. Now that she sees him, all she wants to do is go home to Copenhagen. But it's not as simple as that. She watches as he reaches down to pick something up in front of him on the floor. She can't quite see yet what he's doing. Matthias straightens up and turns to the camera. He's holding out his arm. All of a sudden, in his hand, she sees a kitten. It's gun-metal grey with a white chest. Wriggling like quicksilver. Amara lets out a small laugh. Her mother comes into the living room. She shows her the screen. Matthias is smiling at the camera. The screen is jiggling as the kitten squirms around in his hand. Finally, Matthias lets the kitten go.

'Glædelig jul, Amara,' Matthias says to the camera.

'A cat? Really?' Her mother says.

'Oh, it's a joke between Matthias and me,' Amara

says.

It was a joke. Well, she thought it was only a joke. Except it's not a joke now. Because now there really is a cat. She wants to speak to Matthias. But she hesitates. It's difficult with her mother sitting there. She puts her phone back down. She knows he'll ask her when she's going to come home. She still isn't sure what to say. He hasn't said anything yet about Katrine visiting the house. That's something else they need to talk about. She sits back on the sofa and takes her mother's hand. She squeezes it.

'You're right,' Amara says to her mother. 'Trouble does find me.'

The doorbell rings.

'Oh, that's probably Jesper and his family,' her mother says. 'He said they might come round and see us.'

Amara watches her mother get up to answer the door. She hears her talking. Who is it? Her mother's being formal, polite. She stands and looks towards the door. She sees Matthias in the hallway. Her mother is now bringing him into the living room. He's carrying a cardboard box. Her mother glances at Amara as she walks past them and goes into the kitchen. There's a frown on her face.

'I sent you a video message, did you get it?' Matthias says as he sits on the sofa beside Amara.

Amara nods. She hears a scrabbling of nails on the cardboard box that's now on Matthias's lap. She also hears her mother in the kitchen. The kitchen door's ajar. Amara listens to the conversation. She works out quickly that her mother has dialled her brother. They're talking about her. That Matthias is here.

'Go on,' Matthias says. 'Open the lid.'

Amara pauses. She's distracted. If only Matthias could understand. She doesn't know what to do. She lifts out the kitten. It's warm and wriggly in her hand. She thinks of the skein of geese that flew over the cottage in West Jutland. How they flew in a near-perfect V formation; how one of the geese at the front fell away to the side and slipped to the rear. It rejoined the skein at the back. She knows what happens to birds like that if they don't fly in formation. Her throat feels tight.

Omma's piano

At the traffic lights, Aaron stops. It was always at that very spot on the sidewalk, he would hear Mrs Kim warming up on the piano, notes cascading from her window to sprinkle themselves like delicate fairy dust into the Toronto city air. Usually, she played pieces from the classical Romantics, almost always the Schumanns, more Clara than Robert. He waits for the lights to change. It's been a while since he was last there. He looks up at the second-floor apartment. Mrs Kim's window is wide open. Today, there's only the sound of morning traffic drilling past.

The lights turn green. Aaron's long fingers brush the trunk of the silver maple as he crosses over. In his other hand, he's holding a bunch of white flowers. Michael said to take white. That's the traditional colour when someone dies in the Korean community, he had said. Aaron thinks of the phone call less than a month ago, just after the Victoria Day holiday in May. It was so late in the evening Michael had made a joke. It's either bad news or your lover. It was Jimmy telling him that Mrs Kim had died. Said his mother had something she wanted Aaron to have. Could he come by her apartment?

Aaron had hesitated, his body tense. He said he couldn't. Made some excuse that he was busy. Work. Had to look after Madison, their daughter. Always juggling. Couldn't you mail it? He heard himself say. Michael was lying beside him, not asleep yet. He hissed Who is it? What's going on? Aaron had mouthed the gist of the conversation. Michael said of course he should go meet Jimmy. Oh come on Aaron! His mother has just passed. That's the least you can do for Mrs Kim. Aaron didn't want to explain to Michael why he didn't want to go.

As Aaron hovers outside on the street, the last thing Jimmy had said is going around in his head. He remembers the pause on the phone. As a musician, he knows its significance. A pause in music is an indication that something is going to happen. For a moment, he thought Jimmy had hung up or the line had dropped. But no, Jimmy said something unexpected. I guess you and Michael did get married after all. Aaron quickly turned to look at Michael, who was dozing off. Of course, Aaron said. He didn't get much sleep after that.

Aaron spots a man standing at the apartment window. Must be Jimmy. Too late now to back out. He gives himself thirty minutes. He doesn't want to hang around despite what Michael says. He still has bad memories of the Vincent business, which is what Jimmy was hinting at. He's sure of it. He thought it was all behind him. Mrs Kim must have told Jimmy. But she didn't seem the type. Never one for small talk. It wasn't as if he and Mrs Kim had actually discussed Vincent. It was on the stairs that he had first met Vincent. Aaron was leaving Mrs Kim's. Vincent was waiting to come up. He'd asked if Aaron could give him a hand with a fish tank. Needed two people to lift it. Sure thing, Aaron had said. They'd moved the tank. Vincent offered him a drink and a joint. And then it had started. Their *thing*.

As Aaron walks up the path towards the entrance of the apartment block, he shuts out thoughts of Vincent and the last time he was there. He sees a large rectangular 'For Sale' board with the word 'sold' across it. He wonders if Elinor still lives on the first floor. He glances at the apartment above Mrs Kim's, to Vincent's old apartment on the third. He knows Vincent's gone, bailed out, before the pandemic shut the border between Canada and the USA. Went home to California. Hasn't come back. Aaron's been following him on social media. Last night, he had scrolled through photos of Vincent in Yosemite National Park when Madison was brushing her teeth.

'Look, Papa! A big bear,' Madison had said, pointing at his phone screen, at the grizzly in the background.

But instead of laughing, he had shouted at Madison for getting his phone covered in toothpaste.

At the entrance, Aaron presses the buzzer marked Kim. To the right, there's a bicycle, nestling in the laurel hedge. Metallic red, paint blistering on the cross bar. A voice crackles through the intercom. 'Come on up,

Aaron. It's open.' He leans on the door and pushes. He takes the stairs. Halfway up, there's a slightly built middle-aged man, exhausted looking, the spit of Mrs Kim.

'Hi. You must be Aaron, how are you?' Jimmy says, thrusting out his hand as if grabbing something off a supermarket shelf in a hurry. 'We finally meet. Heard a lot about you. Appreciate you coming by.'

For an uncomfortable moment, the two men stand by the front door. Aaron used to walk straight in but now he hesitates, waiting for Jimmy to step into the apartment first. Jimmy's hands are deep in his jeans pocket, shoulders hunched up to his ears. Aaron gives him the flowers.

'Appreciate it,' Jimmy says. 'Come in. Come in. I used to hear so much about you.'

Aaron notices the nervous repetitions. He follows Jimmy into the apartment. His eyes home in on the far corner of the living room, to the piano by the window overlooking the street. The baby grand, lid open, padded dust protector rolled out across the keys. A beautiful piece. Pianos and people, he always says to Michael, are the same. They have a backstory, a history. But he realises now he had never asked much about Mrs Kim or the piano. All he really knew about her was that she was one of the best teachers in the area. A Schumann nut. Both Schumanns. And always had a wait list to help students get into the music school of their dreams. Except he didn't.

Jimmy stands in the middle of the living room. With his hand, he rubs the back of his head down to the nape of his neck.

'Feels like I'm a burglar going through all her stuff,' Jimmy says, turning to Aaron.

The once vivid orange drapes, tied up with an outsized knot, swing in the breeze.

'Had to get air in here,' Jimmy says finally, pinching his nose.

Aaron's unsettled by the state of Mrs Kim's apartment. It was always, and he's trying to think of the word. Ordered. Yes. Ordered. Like a piano scale. An arpeggio. Always the same. Today, the doors leading off the living area are open. Drawers pulled out, resting at a tilt on runners. Cupboard doors ajar. Lights still on. He remembers the photographs dotted around the apartment. Of Jimmy at his graduations. Mrs Kim had exaggerated the final 's' on the word. Plural. Engineering. Or was it Maths? He can't remember now. Brain freeze. Once or twice, out of politeness, in the early days, Aaron had asked about Jimmy. Coming for a visit? Aaron asked. No. Busy this, busy that, Mrs Kim had replied. It was hard to tell if Mrs Kim was talking about herself or her son. The photographs lie face down ready to be packed up.

'May I?' Aaron says.

'Be my guest,' Jimmy says.

Aaron walks over to the piano. He's hoping Jimmy takes after his mother. In which case, thirty minutes is plenty for Aaron to be back in time to collect Madison from Jelena, their neighbour. It's his turn to do the pickup. He checks the time. Michael always reminds him about the childcare clock that ticks, ticks, ticks. He glances at Jimmy across the living room. He hasn't moved. He looks deep in thought.

With the dust protector off, he pulls out the piano stool and sits. The leather eases with his weight. He adjusts his position, sits tall, hands on the keys. It's a reflex. And thinks back to the Saturday mornings when he used to come, psyched for his lesson, visioning the pieces, practising the finger work in the air as he walked along the street he's just come by. Ignoring the aches and pains in his hands. He had serious dreams about music. Must have been one of Mrs Kim's oldest students. But that was then, he reminds himself quickly as he takes his hands off the piano keys. He's spotted a pile of music, sitting on top of the piano.

He picks the music up and scans the sheets, eyes skimming over Mrs Kim's markings in pencil down the side, usually a single word or two at most. All familiar pieces. He smiles to himself as he comes across Chopin's Ballade No. 4 which made his arms ache; Beethoven's The Tempest was fiendish. Liszt's Rhapsody No. 6? Well, his octave technique always let him down at first, but he got there. So, nothing much has changed at Mrs Kim's.

But for Aaron it has. He's taken his teaching exams. Has a YouTube channel now, teaches online as well as in person. Michael wants him to start piano with Madison. Aaron says he will. But he hasn't. He's decided teaching children isn't his thing. Just plonkity plonk, corrections and all those hovering parents with expectations in their eyes. He's even dabbled in a little composing. Someone made a fortune with a commercial for Nike trainers he'd heard the other day. Aaron wonders what Mrs Kim would make of all that now. He knows the answer.

There's a scrape of a chair from the upstairs apartment. Footsteps. A tap being turned on. Aaron glances quickly at the living room ceiling. Jimmy has walked off to the bedroom. Out of the corner of his eye, Aaron watches him rummaging through drawers, lifting up bedding, looking behind pillows and cushions. He puts the music back down on the piano, thinks about his first meeting with Mrs Kim. Aaron was prepared. He'd done his research on her.

'So, Aaron, who is the greatest classical composer of all times?'

'Robert Schumann,' Aaron had replied, quick as a flash. 'No contest.'

'There is a contest, Aaron,' Mrs Kim said. 'With Clara Schumann. Clara was a child prodigy. Alright, Robert was a genius too,' she conceded, waving her hand. 'Same. Same.'

That's all she wanted to know, that they shared a genuine love of the Schumann couple. A power couple, they had joked. Well, Aaron had joked. A power couple by any modern yardstick. But Mrs Kim didn't take his answers at face value. They had then discussed a selection of pieces, by both Schumanns, in detail. Now, he would have a different kind of conversation. He would ask Mrs Kim what she thought about more contemporary composers he's discovered. He's also drifted into jazz. He looks up and spots the white flowers in a vase, sitting on the piano. He hadn't noticed

Jimmy coming over. He picks the vase up and places it on the music to anchor the sheets down.

'Oh, by the way, I called…' Jimmy says.

He's now in the kitchen, pointing up to the ceiling.

'You know. Apartment 3? I called him. Told him about my mother and a leak from his apartment. Asked him to sort out the repairs as soon as possible. Suppose you saw the sign downstairs. The apartment's just been sold.'

As Jimmy walks towards him, Aaron turns towards the open window. His body tingles with alarm.

'Anyways, he's been here this past week. Packing up. So, it's all worked out,' says Jimmy. 'Saves me a lot of hassle.'

Aaron thinks back to the noises he heard. Not tenants as he had first thought. Been here this past week. Packing up. All his double checking around Vincent has been for nothing. There's a thump from upstairs. Something has dropped on the floor. Through the window, he sees a removal truck parking. He watches it reverse, hazard lights flashing, warning sound beeping. He still has his back to Jimmy, like a dog that faces a wall ignoring the threat.

'Vincent, that's his name. Hope all that noise means he's getting the leak fixed,' Jimmy says. 'Terrible sound proofing. Mom said she could hear everything. And I mean e*verything*. She had some funny nickname for him.'

Aaron turns. Jimmy rolls his eyes when he says *everything*. Aaron knows what the nickname was. It wasn't funny then. It isn't funny now. Perhaps Jimmy means funny strange. Aaron notices that Jimmy's still empty handed. He'd almost forgotten that he's supposed to be collecting something. He takes his phone out of his pocket. There's an urgent text from Michael asking him where Madison's ballet bag is. He quickly replies. *Under the kitchen counter.* And stops himself from adding 'where it always is'. Michael will know something's up with a testy comment like that.

'Omma, sorry Mom, always complained about all the comings and goings upstairs. She said she could recognise who was over. The voices. They had some kind of row. She didn't really say what it was about at first. Eventually said it was about the noise. They ended up not speaking to each other.'

Aaron notices a small smile on Jimmy's face.

'Funny to row about something like that. She never thought her music was ever *that* loud. How could anyone complain about the Schumanns she would always say. And just to annoy him, she started to play that crazy piece. You know, that really loud repetitive one. Played it in the middle of the night, early in the morning.' Jimmy laughs.

Aaron knows exactly what that crazy piece is. It now explains the music when he came here for the last time. He remembers Mrs Kim was playing Chopin instead of something by one of the Schumanns. He heard it at the traffic lights. The unstoppable dazzling stampede of notes came fighting through the small crack of her open window. It was Fall then. She was playing with all the speed and dexterity needed, but with a little too much pedal in Aaron's opinion. Jeez. What a piece to be playing first thing in the morning. Couldn't understand why then. He knows now.

'Chopin's Revolutionary Study,' Aaron says.

'Yeah, that's the one. Chopin. Anyways, I reckon Vincent had some kind of cannabis business going. Always that smell. Notice anything ever when you were…'

Aaron shakes his head, even though Jimmy is right about the cannabis. It was only for recreational use. Helped his playing. Loosened him. Made him relax. It was another reason why he would be at Vincent's. In the lesson with Mrs Kim, all he wanted was for it to end so he could leave and go upstairs to Vincent's apartment. When he was upstairs, he wanted to go home and when he left, he practised and counted the days until Saturday. Music had always been an escape. Its intoxicating alchemy freeing him from the everyday. Then it became a trap, like being caught in an eddy of a fast-flowing river. Which had happened to him once when he was a teenager. He thought he was going to die. He nearly did. He'd also just met Michael. Met him through friends. He'd come back to Toronto. Been working in London. Aaron was still seeing Vincent. Sort of. It was a confusing time. A mess.

Aaron runs his finger along the top of the piano. It clears a line of dust off the black veneer. Marriage. Baby. He never thought he wanted that life. Never thought he could have that kind of life. In some ways, he's never been happier. So, he keeps telling himself and everyone keeps telling him. Michael has asked him to stop smoking because of Madison. He has stopped, well, mostly.

At the window, Aaron is distracted by two men getting out of the removal truck. He hears the rear door rolling up. Jimmy appears at Aaron's side.

'Found it. Here's what I was looking for,' Jimmy says, holding out a large white envelope. 'Actually, it's for both of you.'

Aaron takes it from him. He recognises Mrs Kim's neat, loopy handwriting. She always wrote in HB pencil. *Aaron & Michael.* He spots the ampersand between their names. Could have mailed it, that's for sure, he thinks.

'She was always talking about you and Michael. Really approved of Michael. You know what Mom was like. Always had this ridiculous thing about the Schumanns and their soppy love story.'

Jimmy rolls his eyes. 'As if real life is like that,' he says.

The Schumanns were real life, Aaron says to himself. They'd met very young, fallen madly in love and married against Clara's father's wishes. Mrs Kim had only met Michael the one time. They'd laughed afterwards, agreeing she had definitely been flirting with him.

'She said she was waiting for you to get back in touch once you had decided on your plans,' Jimmy says. 'Said you'd taken a sabbatical from music. Guess it's all worked out, you know.'

Sabbatical? Well, that's one way of describing how he had run away from music. One Saturday he was there at Mrs Kim's. The next gone. And that was how he had sorted out the Vincent business. Except, and he thinks of the sounds coming from upstairs, maybe he hasn't quite. He turns and sees a large truck with a crane pulling up outside. Jimmy turns too.

'Never guess where I found all her meds?' Jimmy says. 'Finally made her go to the doctor. Told her the gingko tea wasn't going to fix her. Took her myself. Found them in here.'

He pats the top of the piano and turns to Aaron.

'That was the only thing that mattered to her,' Jimmy says. 'Mattered more than me, I sometimes thought. Music, I mean. I always felt guilty that I came along and ruined her glittering career. That's why she became a teacher.'

Aaron taps the envelope nervously on the back of his other hand. Michael used to say the same to him about music. Used to call music the third wheel in their marriage.

'I know it wasn't my fault,' Jimmy says.

Aaron watches the men outside on the street talking to each other.

'She wouldn't come live with us. You know that Korean mother-in-law stereotype. Cleans, cooks and takes over? Nope. Not my mom. Said she was always busy this, busy that,' Jimmy says.

The removal men are now looking up at the apartments. Aaron is half listening half watching.

'I called her every day. In the end, she couldn't use the phone. Kept getting confused with the TV remote.'

But Mrs Kim had called Aaron. It was early evening. Probably about two years ago. He recognised the caller

ID. Heard breathing down the phone. She had said a few words he couldn't understand. Must have been Korean. He'd tried to speak to her. In the end, he'd hung up. Later, when they were finally sitting for dinner and Madison was asleep, Michael had asked who it was.

'Wrong number,' Aaron had said.

'Strange, I had a couple of calls like that this week.'

That was something else Jimmy had said when he called. Lucky I found your phone number. Mom had stuck it on the fridge. Never took it down. All the bits of paper and essential paraphernalia of everyday living have been removed. Aaron closes his eyes as he thinks how something so small like hanging up on the phone can now seem so cruel.

'Anyways, as luck would have it, I bumped into Vincent. Just before you arrived. Told him about Mom and that one of her old students was coming over to pick something up. Seemed to know you?' Jimmy says. 'Said sorry to hear about Mom's death. He didn't seem so bad. Made a joke about selling bongs in Venice Beach.'

Sounds like Vincent trying to be funny, Aaron says to himself. Jimmy's phone rings. He glances at Aaron as he answers it.

'Okay,' he says. 'I'll be down right away.'

Jimmy turns.

'Aaron, I'm going to level with you now,' Jimmy says. 'I could have mailed this envelope to you. We both know that. But I wanted you to come by the apartment. Wanted to meet you in fact. Mom always spoke so much about you. Felt almost like...'

Jimmy stops. There are footsteps moving fast on the stairs. Going down, yes. Aaron's sure of it. The door of the apartment block slams.

'I guess I need to get over the fact that I just wasn't the musical one,' Jimmy says, pointing out the window. 'I've been waiting for the removal men. They got delayed. They've come for Omma's piano. Now you're here, maybe you want to stay until the piano has gone?'

Aaron knows he should go. He thinks about how to move a baby grand. It's not difficult. He feels the envelope in his hand and presses it. Its contents are light. Sheet music, he guesses. So much of his music is on an iPad these days. He has that old feeling again, of being caught in an eddy, of being pushed and pulled. He remembers Michael's words: It's the least you can do for Mrs Kim.

'Let me sort a couple of things,' Aaron says to Jimmy, who gives him the thumbs up and walks out of the apartment.

Aaron sends a message to Jelena, asking her if she can hang onto Madison a bit longer. Through the window, he sees Jimmy talking to the removal men on the street. He thinks of his last lesson with Mrs Kim. She had popped her teacup on the piano and sat beside him on a chair. Aaron had his hands on the keys, ready to play. For weeks, his playing was off. He was under prepared, unfocussed. Dreams he'd been chasing, became fragments that kept disappearing around corners. Mrs Kim had picked the music. It was ready on the music stand. A Schumann piece filled with sharps. He had groaned inwardly when he had seen the opening bars.

'Aaron, keep the playing calm,' she said. 'Ease off each phrase. And remember Robert Schumann's instruction? Einfach! Simple.'

Mrs Kim scribbled in the margin in pencil on the music. It wasn't a difficult piece even with the six sharps. And F-sharp major was a beautiful fit for his hands. But Aaron remembers the mistakes. After a short while, she reached for the music and closed it.

'Everyone makes this piece too dramatic. Just play it with tenderness. Otherwise you might as well put on a CD.'

She stood, took the music off the stand and placed it on top of the piano.

'You know, Aaron, if you see an American cockroach in the day, that's when you know you're in trouble,' Mrs Kim said, pointing to the ceiling.

Aaron knew exactly what Mrs Kim was talking about. Or rather who. It was her way of telling him to get his life in order. His life was a mess. He was messing up. She ended the lesson.

'Door's always open,' she had said.

The next day Aaron called Mrs Kim, telling her Michael had seen a bigger apartment. It would be too far to keep crossing town. Said they were talking of getting married and even having a baby.

'If you say so,' Mrs Kim had said. 'Remember Clara Schumann had eight children. Well, seven. Emile died. And none of that got in the way of her music.'

'I'll call you,' Aaron said.

'You'll be busy this, busy that,' Mrs Kim said. 'And

remember, Aaron, you don't decide when to leave music. Music leaves you.'

He was at the bottom of the eddy. He'd blocked Vincent's number. Went cold turkey. It was the only way out. Aaron sits back down at the piano. His hands flutter above the keyboard, muscle memory kicking in. He plays the Schumann piece in his head. He knows exactly how to play it now. Then, he didn't. Couldn't.

There's a knock at the apartment door. Jimmy opens it. It's one of the removal men.

'We're all ready to get started,' he says to Jimmy.

Jimmy turns to Aaron. 'Ready?'

Aaron quickly checks his phone. There's a video from Jelena of Madison in the garden painting. With a smiley emoji. He messages Michael to tell him he's running late. *Just helping with Mrs Kim's piano.* Michael messages immediately back. *Getting paid? $$$.* He hopes Michael's joking. Aaron knows what will happen to the piano. First, the music rack will be taken off, then the centre leg with pedals and the remaining legs. They all get wrapped up. The lid is closed. Then padding. The piano gets tilted on its side before it's taken away. And in its place is dust and the forgotten detritus of day to day living on the floor such as gum wrappers, buttons, paper clips, dead flies, old biro pens.

The removal men come into the apartment. Aaron stands and goes to the side of the piano. He takes the rod from the lid and slots it in its place. He holds the lid in both hands, with upturned palms, across the span of his fingers, and lets it descend slowly. Jimmy stands back. They watch until the piano is padded, strapped and ready to go.

'I'm sorry for your loss,' he says to Jimmy, when the piano is on its side, ready for the next stage.

It's as awkward to leave as it was to step into the apartment. Jimmy and Aaron stand side by side for a few moments, watching the removal men work. After a few moments, Jimmy turns and gives Aaron a fist bump.

'Door's always open,' he says. 'That's what Omma always used to say.'

As he stands at the door, he rubs the back of his neck again.

'You know, she wasn't a huggy kind of mom. But she was a good mom.'

Aaron nods. He knows what Jimmy's saying. He walks out of the apartment, taking the envelope with him. He crosses back over to the other side of the street. The removal men are moving fast. He waits by the silver maple. Out of the corner of his eye, a bicycle passes. He turns his head to follow it. The cyclist takes a left up the path Aaron has just walked down. Stops, dismounts and pushes the bicycle into the hedge. It's Vincent. He's timed his return perfectly, Aaron thinks. *Too* perfectly.

Above his head, in mid-air, looming, swaddled in its protective green quilted cover, stripped of all its majesty, Aaron sees Mrs Kim's piano. The removal men stand below, looking up, their hands across their foreheads shielding their eyes from the late morning sun. Jimmy is leaning out of the window, watching as the piano moves through the wide opened windows and into the morning air. The piano is held by steel wire. The crane lifts it high and through the air. There are whistles, instructions and shouts to the crane operator. A small group of people gather across the street.

Aaron thinks of Madison. He'll tell her all about Mrs Kim's piano. He'll make it into a bedtime story. He'll change bits around and include a mouse who comes out at night and jumps on the piano keys, playing music by the Schumanns. Both Schumanns. Robert and Clara.

'Sorry folks,' one of the removal men says. 'It'll only take a few more minutes.'

'But this is making me late,' a woman says.

'Someone's died,' the removal man says.

'Who?'

'Just an old lady,' the removal man says.

Mrs Kim's piano has now been lowered to street level. It stands there on its trolley. The removal men move it to line up with the back of the truck. They wave everyone on, saying it's safe from falling pianos. Aaron watches as the body of the piano is pushed up the ramp. Lodged. Secured with ropes. The removal men give it a shove. It's rock solid. People start to drift off.

Aaron messages Michael to say he's on his way home. He'll go past Loblaws, the grocery store, and pick up food. They're out of yoghurt, milk and cereal. Aaron starts to walk. He's worked out what's in the envelope. Which piece of music Mrs Kim has given him and Michael, with all her markings in pencil still on it. He's sure it's Schumann's Romance Opus 28, No. 2, composed by Robert for Clara, the year of their marriage.

'Aaron, let the notes rise and fall. I want to hear every note. This is a love song,' Mrs Kim had said, tapping the music with the end of her pencil.

You're right Mrs Kim, Aaron says to himself. It is a love song. But even Clara and Robert had their problems. It wasn't all cutesy and writing each other love messages in their shared diary. Robert had died, locked up in a psychiatric asylum; Clara had to keep the family show on the road all on her own, working herself to the bone, overshadowed by a coterie of male composers and performers.

He looks up at the sky. Planes crisscross, leaving tangled milky white contrails. He realises he's forgotten to ask Jimmy a question. He doesn't know where Mrs Kim's piano is going. He'll call. Then he remembers he'd said that once to Mrs Kim. He was hoping he was going to feel better after coming to Mrs Kim's. But he doesn't.

He pauses.

Light of my eye

From my seat in the foyer, I watch people come and go. I hear Hebrew and English weaving through the chilled air. Hotels are hungry for business since the last missile attacks in Israel. Prosperity can dangle like a thread here. As I wait, I spot today's newspaper that's been sitting on the small round coffee table in front of me. I scan the headlines about the upcoming elections and the start of another peace process. Everyone knows you can't talk about Israel without mentioning the situation and politics. They're like conjoined twins. The situation, it's a euphemism. It's conflict. War. It's been like this for years and years. And everyone takes sides.

When I first came to Israel in my twenties, I would never have imagined returning and sitting in a swanky beachside hotel in Tel Aviv. I hadn't planned to come to this conference. It was a last-minute decision. Someone had a passport problem. So, I stepped in to be a panellist at a global conference on trauma. I'm a consultant trauma surgeon in one of London's biggest and busiest hospitals. I attended with clinical psychologists and psychiatrists, professors of neuroscience, holistic healers, members of the Polyvagal Institute and a peace charity. Trauma is big business these days.

Thirty years ago, I came to Israel to work on a kibbutz. It was the thing to do then. I was a hospital doctor ready to jack it all in. I'd made a mistake. The patient had underlying problems that I'd missed on her records. I lost my nerve after that. I had a summer to think about what I wanted to do with my life. I found a kibbutz close to the Jordanian border, in the Beit She'an valley. I was seduced by pictures of citrus groves, of teams of young kibbutzniks carrying baskets of picked fruit in bright yellow sunshine. I met Sarah at the kibbutz. She wasn't a volunteer like me. She was part of the kibbutz family. What I really mean to say is in the summer of 1993, I fell in love.

The conference ended yesterday. I'm on my way home, getting picked up by taxi to go to the airport and catch my flight. As I'm waiting, I take out my phone. It's the first time I've had a few minutes to myself. The strange thing is that being back here now in Israel is like poking a dying fire. Memories are coming back to life. I quickly type the name of the kibbutz into the search engine. It comes up straightaway. I click on the website. And click again to translate the website from Hebrew to English. I scroll through photos on the homepage. The kibbutz has changed. Of course, it has. It's got bigger. They even take paying guests now.

I see familiar faces in the photos. Moshe, he looks

older. I worked with Moshe in the fish farms. Looks like he works in the office now. I zoom in. Yes, he's wearing a shirt. He'll hate working indoors. Oh, and there's Ruth, Moshe's wife. And Eytan, their son. I peer closely at the photo. He was only a young boy when I knew him. He has his arms around a couple of children. They must be his! That's impossible. Of course, it isn't. I hover over the Contact tab to get the telephone number. If I call, I know they'll remember me. They'll remember me because of Sarah's accident. But I don't know if Sarah's still there. That's who I'm really looking for.

Above the hubbub in the hotel, I hear my name being called. The words Daniel Chatterton echo through the marble foyer. It's a woman's voice. I put my hand up to say I'm here. I turn my head. I see a young woman from the hotel reception waving at me. She comes over. She tells me that they've been advised by Security that any guest leaving today for the airport must allow more time than usual. The roads will be slower. The airport will have additional security. There's a delegation flying into Israel to meet with the Government. There'll be delays everywhere. My taxi has been rescheduled. All the details are there, she says, handing me a piece of paper.

Being called like that reminds me of how I first met Sarah at the kibbutz. I can picture her now. But it was her voice I heard first. As I went in for breakfast in my first week, I heard Sarah's voice soaring across the vaulted roof of the communal refectory where everyone gathered for meals. Sarah was in charge of the kitchens.

She was welcoming all the new volunteers. The way she said my name was like a songbird with her Hebrew-accented English. Shalom, Dr Daniel! Shalom, shalom! Sarah was wearing dungarees. Of course, she was. That's what all the photos were like of kibbutz life, this collective ideal of socialist dreams and desires.

For me, it was ideal for a time. There was something comforting about the physicality of life on the kibbutz. I think of Moshe again, office-bound now, a bear of a man. He took me under his wing. He worked me hard. We threw the fishing nets so that the rope edge landed on the water's surface in a circle, sending concentric ripples outwards. Slowly we walked the net in, trapping the fish—the carp, the tilapia—then we dragged the net's ever-increasing weight to the pond's edge. When you work in the fish farms, the day finishes before breakfast. That's when most of the other work begins on the kibbutz. In some ways, working in the fish farms was like being a hospital doctor. I worked through the nights and early morning before the sun rose. Sometimes I was up at midnight, at other times three in the morning, depending on which team I was in. But it was also different. If I made a mistake, it wasn't a matter of life and death. It was just what I needed then. To be in a bubble. To be away. To feel free.

I store the number for the kibbutz on my phone. All of a sudden, I think of Benny. I haven't seen him in any photos on the website. It didn't take him long to come up to me in the refectory. Actually, he squared up to me. He was built like a bulldog, as tall as he was wide. Frightened the hell out of me. He'd just finished a tour of the Golan Heights. You need to know something about Sarah, he said. And walked off. It was like being hit by a bullet train. Bang! He must have noticed how much time we were spending together, Sarah and me. We were soon together every second we weren't working. We got into this routine of meeting up in the hot afternoons when she had finished in the kitchens. But very quickly, there were requests for me to help with something or other, to keep me away from the refectory. The subtext was: away from Sarah. But I didn't listen. I didn't pay attention to any of the warnings.

I read the message that's just been handed to me, to double check the changed arrangements. The taxi driver, Amir, will arrive at noon instead of 1.30pm. I look for the newspaper that was on the coffee table in front of me. Someone has taken it. I check my watch. It's only a few minutes now until my pickup time. Beside me is a small bag of pomegranates. I bought them at the Carmel Market earlier this morning. Sarah taught me a few words of Hebrew. The strange thing is that the word for pomegranate is the same as the word for grenade. Rimmon. I remember that now. The pomegranates remind me of when Sarah came to find me in the shade of one of the small orchards. She pulled a pomegranate off a tree. I watched her take out a knife from the pocket of her dungarees and make a deep cut in the fruit. She pulled the fruit apart with her thumbs, to expose the crimson interior. As she came up to me, she offered me a half.

I pick up one of the pomegranates I bought and hold

it in my hand. I feel its leathery skin, how hard it is to push my thumb into and tear it apart. Together, Sarah and I ate the pomegranate, seed by seed, sitting in the orchard. It's one of the slowest fruits to eat. Now I realise why Sarah had chosen it, why we had to sit there for so long eating it. She needed to ask me a question. And she needed time to ask it. Daniel, are you leaving soon? I said I was but I hadn't a plan. Will you come with me? I asked. She didn't answer me. She said she had to go to work.

A few weeks later, as the summer was coming to an end and my time was finishing at the kibbutz, I was still waiting for Sarah's answer. On the day before I was leaving, Sarah appeared in the half light of dusk. I was packing up the motorbike ready to head south of the Galilee and beyond. Sarah had with her a small bag on her back, a leather jacket and her arm looped through the strap of a bike helmet. She handed me her things.

Where do you want to go? she asked.

Jerusalem, I said.

From where I'm sitting, I see a line of taxis through the windows. I'm looking out for Amir, the taxi driver. Leaving earlier is a good thing, come to think of it. I must be home tonight. I told Gabriel I would definitely be back for the weekend. Whilst I've been waiting, I've been thinking of making a call to the kibbutz. Time's running out. My phone's still in my hand. I look at the floor to ceiling windows of the hotel foyer. I've learnt from my work that physical injuries from bomb blasts are usually from glass. Shards of glass that can slice

131

through skin like butter. That's what normally kills people, the glass. But it's the after effects that are the most painful and damaging, the psychological, the emotional. As doctors, we talk about the scorecard of our bodies, how they keep count of the trauma and its effect. Trauma can last years. It can also pass through generations. As a surgeon, I am one of the first professionals to treat a trauma victim. I'm the one that says, hello, I'm Dan, I'm a doctor, I'm going to look after you. I rarely have contact with a patient later to see how they've really recovered.

After Sarah's accident, I cut short my time in Israel. I went back to England. And back to medicine. I pleased my parents. I kept what happened to Sarah to myself. I wanted to be in touch. I wrote Sarah a letter. I played the 'what if' game for a while, imagining if we met again, what might happen. I waited for a reply. I stopped waiting. I never heard back. I felt guilty after the accident. I still feel guilty as if in some way it was my fault. If I had listened to Benny, if I had never asked her to come to Jerusalem, the accident wouldn't have happened. Soon, work and life took me over. And later, I met Gabriel's mother.

Through the window, a driver steps out of his taxi and waves at me. It must be Amir. I obviously look like someone waiting to go to the airport. I put my phone back in my pocket, pick up my things and head out of the hotel entrance quickly.

'Dr Daniel,' Amir calls across to me. 'Dr Daniel! Marhaba!'

I return the greeting in Arabic. It's a shock, the

outside heat. I feel it on my back as I walk towards the taxi and get in. We wait to pass through the security gate of the hotel to turn on to HaYarkon Street. The traffic is slow moving.

'Eh, what's happening! It's Friday,' Amir says. 'Yalla! Hurry up!'

Friday is the holy day for Muslims. It's Shabbat for Jews. The traffic would normally be quieter.

'It's all in the news,' I say, remembering the newspaper headlines. 'A delegation from the USA coming for talks. Extra security.'

'Makes no difference. Everyone still drives crazy here.'

With years of conflict, daily tensions rise quickly. They say you can feel it everywhere, in the traffic, how people queue, speak to each other, argue. Before I came, a colleague in London told me Tel Aviv is a bubble, somehow protected from the rest of the conflict in Israel. But I'm not so sure. I remember a newspaper report that said Iran could send a missile and hit the city in seven minutes. That's not living in a bubble.

These past few days, I've been in a hotel kind of bubble. As I leave, it makes me think of Jerusalem and the short time Sarah and I had. We stayed in the Old City at a small pensione with a roof-top terrace. We joked and said that this was our five-star Hotel King David. We looked over the stretched, elongated panorama of the sun-baked city. We drank coffee flavoured with cardamom. Ate felafels from the Yemenite Jew's stall. Jerusalem was dry, hot and dusty. The Dome of the Rock, its golden dome like a jewel, shimmered as the sun went down. We watched the sunset each evening. I remember once someone came up onto the roof. The door opened and closed softly. Whoever it was knew there was no room for them.

I distract Amir from the traffic and ask him if he's married. He points at a photograph, hanging down from his driving mirror. I see a woman and three children.

'That's my wife,' Amir says. 'Very good cook. Makes very good fattoush.'

He brakes suddenly, raising his hands in frustration.

'And my sons. Very clever. Speak excellent Hebrew. Don't believe all Arab boys use slingshots.' He laughs. 'Makes no difference. Once an Arab always an Arab.'

After only a few minutes, we come to another standstill. Amir looks at me in the driver's mirror.

'You married, Dr Daniel?'

'Divorced. One son,' I say.

'Ah, so you understand the problem here in Israel. We are like a couple that don't get along. But we have one child, who we can't divide into two.'

That's Amir's way of talking about the situation, that it's like an unhappy couple. I should know. I've done divorce and co-parenting of Gabriel. It wasn't easy. And Jerusalem is what's at stake. How to divide a city? How to share a city? Even though it's already been shared for centuries. Amir looks at me again in the mirror. The tacit mention of Jerusalem has been an ice breaker of sorts.

'So, what do you think of Israel? Crazy, eh?'

'Every country has its crazies,' I say to him.

I'm not going to take sides. Anyone who reads a newspaper, headlines, online accounts, knows about Israel. Everyone's touched and has been touched by death because of the situation. Death awaits us all. I know, as a doctor, most people want an ordinary death. A death at home. But death isn't always ordinary. When Sarah and I met, we were both dealing with death. We only realised that about each other when we got to Jerusalem.

One morning, it was early, probably our second or third day, I was stroking Sarah's back. We were talking after we'd just made love. Sarah asked me again why I'd come to Israel. I finally told her about the patient who'd died. I told her everything, how I had made a mistake. It was my first real experience of death as a doctor. I said I had come to Israel because I needed to get away. Don't throw away your career over something like that, everyone told me. What's done, is done.

Sarah said to me that Israel was a strange place to come to in those circumstances. I asked her why she'd come away with me. I wasn't expecting her to. Lying, stretched out, naked, long, I stroked her back, from the base of her spine to her neck. It was like playing the piano without playing a note. She told me she needed to get away like me. From the claustrophobia of the kibbutz. Everyone wanted to help her but there was nothing they could do. Everyone knew what was best for her, what she needed. And Jerusalem, and me, it promised her a chance to vanish for a while.

Sarah rolled over onto her back, not to look at me,

but to look somewhere more in the distance. I'm a widow, she said. A widow at twenty-three years old. The word hung heavily in the air between us. A widow she said again. She told me Tomer had died. Killed. He was in a tank. In the armoured division. He was caught as he was coming back over the border. No one survived the attack. Sarah shifted, her face resting now on the backs of her hands. Anyway, war is normal here, she said. I knew Tomer had died. I knew it had happened. Before they came to the house. Before the knock on the door. I felt it in my body. She also told me about the row with Tomer before he left. Then, she asked me a question. Daniel, have you always felt safe? You know, as a child? I said I did. Always.

But it wasn't really Tomer she wanted to talk about. She said she needed to tell someone like me, an outsider, how frightened she'd always felt. She told me how she didn't know anything different from war. Her father had fought in the Six Day War. Her younger brother was doing his military service. She said she was frightened of everything. It's like being in the dark. You put the light on. But you still feel frightened.

Amir's tapping his window to get my attention, to look at something. The traffic has come to another standstill. 'See.'

I know what he's telling me to look at. I've already spotted them. A group of men and women, Israeli Defence Force soldiers in olive green uniforms, manning a street security point. They're heavily armed with semi-automatic pistols in holsters, and rifles in their hands. I've seen what weapons like that can do.

And rubber bullets. The soldiers can't be much out of their teens. Like Gabriel. Responsibility for life and death in the hands of the very young. I remember that was me all those years ago. They also remind me of Benny. At the kibbutz, he was volatile and threatening, a coiled spring. I understand him better now through my work as a doctor.

Amir's still pointing at the soldiers. We're all waiting for something. He's gone quiet. My body has stiffened. The soldiers turn in our direction. They look at us. They say something to each other and two walk towards us, a short distance and I'm counting every step. One of the soldiers bends to see into the taxi. Amir keeps his hands on the steering wheel. When the soldiers step back, I notice how my muscles have clamped in my neck and shoulders. It's a similar feeling to when I'm expecting a code red at the hospital. The expectation. The uncertainty. The adrenaline starts. I'm usually clicking my biro. Deep in thought. Waiting. Catching the eyes of the team who are waiting too. Alert. Energy levels rising. But it's cortisol that's coursing through my body now.

'Crazy, I'm just a taxi driver. I only want to work, go home, and look after my olive trees,' Amir says.

The soldiers wave us on.

It's Amir's turn to change the subject. I'm glad he has. 'So, tell me where you've been?'

'Nowhere this time. Not even the beach. But last time, I went to many places.'

I tell him about the kibbutz. How I worked on the land. Amir jokes. He calls me a fellahin. A peasant, he says! He asks me what my parents thought about me wasting my education doing something like that.

'I went to Jerusalem,' I say, instead of answering the question.

'Have you seen the wall?'

At first, I'm confused. I think he means the Western Wall in Jerusalem's Old City, the one that always flashes up on the news. But he doesn't. I know what he's talking about. I've seen pictures of the West Bank Wall. I've seen photos of Gaza too. Barriers that are meant to create safety and security for some, hatred and division for others. They're all over the world. I've seen the Berlin Wall, now filed down to a keloid scar that zigzags through the city. But I don't want to talk about Jerusalem. I don't want to talk about the situation and politics. I know Jerusalem's like a pressure cooker. For a short time, the situation never touched Sarah and me. We could pretend it wasn't happening. We had created a world of our own. We were in our own bubble.

'Then I travelled,' I say, moving the conversation away from Jerusalem.

'The Dead Sea? It's full of sinkholes now,' Amir says. 'And Masada? You don't need to walk up. There's a cable car all the way to the top. A made in Switzerland cable car!'

I hear a song on the radio. I listen for a few moments. I know it well. I tap my fingers on my knee to the beat. It was playing all the time in Jerusalem when Sarah and I were there. I ask Amir about the song.

Amir says something in Arabic. 'You know what

that means?'

He's looking at me in the mirror. I shake my head. He says it again.

'My darling, light of my eye. That's the title of the song. Egyptian singer. In our language, you say light of my eye to someone you love very much. Who's precious to you like your wife, your child,' he says.

Light of my eye, I say to myself. The song was playing in taxis, in cafés, on car radios, in shops. We were listening to it without ever understanding its words, all those years ago. Never even talked about it. I look out of the window as we drive through the city. The mention of Masada takes me back to the high barren mountainous plateau on the edge of the Judean desert. It was the last place we went before the accident. Masada is an ancient stone fortress. The path winds like a snake up the steep sides of the mountain that crumbles like a cake. It's shaley, rocky and exposed to the elements.

Part way up, as we walked to the top, Sarah pointed to the view. It was smudgy, the wind kicking up the dust. The Dead Sea was ribboned with a border of salt. It's the lowest point on earth. Jordan, Sarah had said, pointing to the Moab mountains in the East as the hot summer wind rifled through her hair. To the north, Daniel, can you see Syria? To the South, there's Egypt. And to the West, the Mediterranean and Europe. I followed where she was pointing. Where you're from, Sarah had said to me. Over there. Where you're going back to. She had sounded so clear. So definite. So sure. Telling me I was going home.

Sarah's accident happened straight after we had walked down from the fortress. We were intending to head south. Towards Eilat. Or I thought we were. I have gone over the accident many times, starting with the typical logical and rational thinking of a doctor. I was experienced, careful, aware of the risks. With Sarah as my passenger, I adjusted to the added weight and the road conditions. It was hot. I'd checked the tyre pressure. There was dust from the Judaean desert, but I had allowed for that.

The Friday traffic is flowing better now. We turn onto the main highway, Route 1, which will take us to Ben Gurion airport. Amir says something to me. He's playing me some other music. He's turned the volume up. He shouts another singer's name. I don't catch it.

'From Syria,' he says, his finger jabbing at the radio.

I nod back at him. It would have been the easiest thing in the world for me and Sarah's family to have blamed the accident on something else: a goat that had wandered onto the road; a lorry driver speeding his way up from the south with Lebanese pop blaring, an evil eye swinging from the mirror. And I did for a while. We were tired after our climb. I had turned the throttle on the bike, to speed up. I wanted to drive in daylight. After a few minutes, I felt the bike shift on the road. The loss of balance. I knew instantly what had happened. There was no sound. It's how children drown. Sliding down through the water in silence.

I braked and skidded. Cars stopped. They called the ambulance services. I told everyone I was a doctor. That

140

Sarah needed to get to hospital fast. I stroked her. I kept her warm. Told her I loved her, that her family loved her, that she was safe. That was all she needed to know. I went with her to the hospital. I called the kibbutz. Her family came as fast as they could. They thanked me. I said that Sarah was exhausted from the trip. That she must have been drowsy on the back of the bike. They told me I needn't stay. They thanked me for saving Sarah's life. Any doctor will tell you what really saves a life in a motorbike accident. It's the protective gear. The helmet. The jacket. It was Benny who had saved Sarah's life. Not me. He had given the gear to Sarah. I wonder if he knows that.

Ben Gurion airport is up ahead. I see the signs. Amir drives towards the drop-off lane. We both get out of the taxi and shake hands.

'Shukran, my friend,' Amir says.

We slap each other across the back as if we've come through some long, risky journey. I thank him and wish him good luck.

'Inshallah,' Amir says. God willing. 'You people, you think it is just a real estate problem.'

That's Amir. With the final word on the situation. I'm in good time as I head through the departure hall and security. I check my flight. No delays. But there are slow moving queues. I put my luggage through the scanner. I walk through. I get patted down. My passport is inspected. I'm checked again. I head through to airside. I listen to my voicemail messages. As I hear the first one, I smile. It's from Gabriel. He's reminding me about the weekend. I hadn't forgotten. We have plans.

He's got tickets to something or other. I listen to the next message. Yes, yes, I nod. It's a friend. Dinner Sunday night? When you're divorced, Sunday night is a lonely time. I message to say thanks. See you then. And can I bring anything? I know what I'll bring. Those pomegranates. Except, when I look around, I realise I've left them behind. They're sitting in the back of Amir's taxi.

As I wait for my flight to board, I think about the conversation with Amir. The conversation about the situation. He's right. It's always about Jerusalem. It was all about Jerusalem for Sarah and me. And the accident? I'd always told myself that Sarah was exhausted by the heat and had fallen off. But now, feeling the tension that goes with living here, sifting through memories, talking with Amir, I'm not so sure. I think that Sarah may have let go. There was no other vehicle involved. No twists and turns on the road. I can still feel her hands around my waist, her fingers unlocking, one by one, as she released herself, her weight shifting. But I'll never know for sure.

I take my phone out and search for the song that reminds me of Jerusalem. I type in the English translation. It comes up. I read the Arabic. Habibi, ya nour el ein. No, I decide not to listen to it. I click again on the kibbutz website. I search the photo gallery slowly looking at each photo. I'm looking for Sarah. One more time, I tell myself. But I still can't find her. I glance outside. I'll be leaving before sunset. Before Shabbat. I start to imagine the phone call. The phone rings in the office. It'll be Sarah who'll answer it. And

142

I'll say, it's Daniel from a long time ago, and Sarah will say, Shabbat Shalom, Daniel. Mah shlomchah? How are you? And I will say. Metzuyan. Great.

I'll then explain about the medical conference, how I've been staying in a swanky hotel and eating felafels with a knife and fork. She'll laugh. We'll both be thinking of our time in Jerusalem. But it's one of those imagined conversations that doesn't go anywhere. It fades quickly and disappears. It's time to let it all go. I think of Moshe. Moshe was always right when he talked about the situation. Daniel, we must look ahead. Not back. I won't make the phone call. But I can still picture Sarah now. See her smiling. She's happy. Yes. She's happy. That's how I want to remember her.

I spot the plane, sitting on the runway, air bridge connected. It's being refuelled, the luggage loaded. I'll head soon to the final security check. I think of Amir, the walls, the young soldiers with their guns, the helmet and jacket that saved Sarah's life. All those things we have to protect ourselves. But they don't protect us. Not really.

Que tengas suerte

I can't breathe. Mamá! Get him away from me. Mamá! José! Help me.

It's three in the morning. Woodie checks the time. He's in the bathroom getting ready. He switches off the light and walks quietly in his socks to the front door. Why did Sissy make me take this job? Bring ID, they said. Security is tight. Woodie pats his shirt pocket. He puts his boots on and looks back up the corridor. Opens the front door. The cold Arizona night air rushes in.

'Have a good one, Woodie!' a voice calls out.

'Jeez, don't you ever sleep?' Woodie says. 'See you later, Sissy. Just off to work. I'll be back around lunch time. You take care.'

'You take care. It's a cold one. Oh...'

There's a pause.

'Don't mess up! And...'

Woodie finishes his sister's sentence. And remember we need the money. Why can't Sissy keep off my back?

Always reminding me as if I need reminding. He steps out onto the porch and shuts the door quietly behind him. He breathes in the night air as he walks to the station wagon parked on the driveway. He gets in, slips the gearshift into drive.

As he pulls away, Woodie turns on the radio and surfs the channels to find the news:

Two more bodies have been found. With the temperatures dropping, we expect to find more. It's tough out there in the Sonoran Desert. Cold at night. Hot in the day. And not a drop of water. Expect more border police over the next few weeks.

Halfway into his journey, Woodie slows and looks out the car window. On the edge of the Sonoran Desert, he sees the outline of saguaro cacti. Tall, spiny, with their arms held high, like giants surrendering. They scare him, always have done. The darkness scares him too. He tilts his head to the dusting of silver stars in the night sky. He'd better not be late. Being early is good, Sissy always says. She told him it's a good job. Well, it's a goodish job. He needs the money what with Sissy being as she is. Her medical bills. No medical insurance. It's his turn now to look after her.

A mile out, Woodie sees the sign, in the pitch black, with its under lighting. Just like the famous Hollywood sign he's seen on the TV. Detention Center. Real weird, Woodie says to himself. Nothing but Arizona desert and sun-parched scrub land here. His stomach churns. He taps his fingers on the steering wheel as he remembers the directions again. Make a right after El Diablo café. He's passing the café now. He sweeps around to take the road heading east. There's the next sign. It says 'Welcome'. He's almost there. Everything looks different in the dark. Everything is different in the dark.

Ahead, Woodie spots a building, its outer walls topped by curling razor wire. He parks in the car lot. There's only one word to describe what he's looking at, and that's prison. He hasn't changed his mind even though he was told at the interview it isn't a prison. It's a detention center. Different. Purpose built for illegal aliens. But it looks like a prison. A dog barks. The sound bounces off the rocks and hillside into the dark. Better keep away from me, buddy, Woodie says to himself.

Even though he's early, Woodie gets out of the car and walks across to the security booth. He hands his ID over to Earl, the security officer. Woodie's read the name already on his badge. The barrier lifts. Earl lets Woodie through. He walks up to the front office. He does it all over again. This time Kurt checks him out on the computer. Next, in the lobby, there's a scanner. He slides his pocket contents through the X-ray machine. It reminds Woodie of how he used to case a supermarket, checking where all the security was positioned—people, cameras, alarms, sensors, you name it. The next set of doors slide open. He walks through. He's at the reception. Woodie glances at the wall opposite him. It's filled with handcuffs and restraints hanging in rows. Last time, he didn't count them. Now he does. But, as he counts, he's interrupted by a voice.

'Over here, William Hardwood!'

Woodie turns and sees Raquel, his new boss. She

interviewed him a few weeks back. She waves at him with both hands and waddles across the room. She rattles and jangles, weighed down at her hips by a heavy belt.

'Here's hoping we don't need to use those on you!' she says, pointing at the handcuffs.

'Yes, ma'am. If my cleaning ain't up to scratch, you just tell me.'

That's what Sissy says. Just suck up if you need to.

'So, here's the thing, William Hardwood,' Raquel says. 'I need you to work fast here. Floors first. Latrines next. Garbage last. That'll take you most of the morning. Keep your head down. Our residents won't mess with you unless they think you're an immigration lawyer. Then they'll be all over you like some latino pop star.' She laughs loudly. '¿Hablas un poco español?' Do you speak a little Spanish?

Woodie makes a small measurement with his finger and thumb.

'Poquito,' Raquel says. 'That's okay. A poquito is plenty. We've mostly got women and children here. Family units. Some unaccompanied minors. Got to process them later today. In here, life is complicated. Muy complicada. Just do your job. We're in the business of keeping people safe and alive. Better here than out there.'

She jabs her finger towards the front entrance.

Are we there yet? No. When will we be there? No sé. I don't know.

Time drags during his first shift. Woodie hasn't even seen a fly yet. If a fly can't get in, then it really is a prison, no matter what anyone says. But Woodie's seen feet, lots of feet in flip flops, in sneakers, walking across his floors. He thinks of them already as *his* floors rather than the floors. That hasn't taken long, only an hour or two. The feet come across his floor with a slow tired 'I've got all day' kind of rhythm. Sometimes, there's an extended palm out to him to say perdón! Sorry. Sorry for the footprints across your clean floor.

Towards the end of the morning, Woodie realises he's forgotten the garbage. That's the last thing he has to do before he can finally go home. Raquel told him that. He gathers up his cleaning gear and hurries to the janitor's office. Inside, he spots two large trash cans. He lifts the lid off one and looks in. That's not garbage. He lifts off the other lid. Same again. Not garbage either. The contents are what he and Sissy would try and sell at a car boot sale. On the floor beside the trash cans, Woodie notices a small business card. It must have fallen out when he was emptying the garbage. There's the face of a man, a smiling face, staring up at him on the card. He picks it up off the floor. It's a priest, in a cassock. Arcipreste Oscar Romero. Who the heck is he? Sissy will know, especially if he's famous or dead. He slips the card into his pocket.

'All good, señor Janitor?' a voice behind him says.

Woodie spins round. It's Raquel.

'Getting through what you need to get through?' she asks.

Woodie points at the trash cans. His heart has

speeded up.

'Is this garbage?' he says.

'Well, that depends. We can't let our residents keep this stuff. But we don't keep any of it either.'

Raquel turns to walk out and then stops.

'Listen up, William Hardwood,' she says. 'We have more of these people heading our way. Dumped by their coyote in the desert without a sip of water. Lucky they survived the night in our hostile terrain. Many don't survive. And we don't find them for months and months. Sometimes never. Sometimes we find a few bones after they've cooked to death without water. That's a real bad death.' Raquel is still leaning against the door. 'How long do you reckon someone can survive in our desert without water, William?'

Woodie remembers the news bulletin he heard coming in to work on the radio. He shrugs.

'Two days. Maybe three. And that's if they're healthy. Not if they've been riding that devil of a freight train for days on end. Which they probably have,' Raquel says. 'So that's what happens when you dream of a better life. Una vida mejor. In someone else's back yard. But we ain't responsible for dreams in here.'

Raquel claps her hands to get his attention.

'Let's get this show on the road,' she says. 'And yes, it's all garbage.'

He's heard her loud and clear. Oscar Romero? Woodie pats his pocket. He's going to check that priest dude out the minute he gets home.

Irene has a song in her head. She feels the rhythm of

the freight train. Someone punches her arm. It's José.

It doesn't take Woodie more than a week to learn the routine. As long as it doesn't require schoolbooks, he's always been a quick learner. He only pretends to be an idiot to avoid attention, things he doesn't like doing, people he doesn't want to mix with. It's always worked for him. He greets the women and children. He nods at Earl and Kurt as he checks in. And he's getting used to Raquel telling the same joke, the one about the handcuffs. And each morning Woodie says the same thing back.

Today, as he switches off his car engine in the parking lot and sits there a moment, he's trying to remember the new joke Raquel told him yesterday. He clears his throat, just as Raquel does. He puts his hands on his hips, just as Raquel does.

'So, William Hardwood. Here's one for you to ponder on this morning. What does the President of the United States of America and an illegal alien have in common?'

Woodie now plays himself, pretending he doesn't know the answer to the question. 'I don't know, ma'am, I really don't know,' he replies.

'Well, I'll tell you.' Woodie pauses just like Raquel. 'They both ride in the Beast.'

Woodie remembers Raquel roaring with laughter, her head back, mouth open wide like a double barn door. She repeated the punchline. They both ride in the Beast. He saw her silver cavities. She has a lot of cavities. He can picture Raquel standing there, legs spread-eagled, belly heaving as she laughed. Big, tall and sturdy like a saguaro cactus. But he still doesn't get the joke. He'll have to check it out with Sissy.

But, Oscar Romero, Saint Oscar Romero. He knows who he is. Woodie found him on the Internet. Did that the minute he got home. Didn't need to ask Sissy. Didn't want to ask her or she would have asked him questions like, where the heck did he get that card from. It was clear as day who the priest was. Famous and dead. That's for sure. Shot. Murdered. In San Salvador. A good man, from all accounts. It just doesn't make sense, Woodie says to himself, to keep a card of a saint, a good person, in your pocket. Then you get locked up. And even though you're not in prison, you have to throw away the few things you've packed and travelled far with. It's not like they're bad people. Not like they've stolen anything. Not like me. Now, I probably did deserve to go to prison, but I got lucky. That's one thing he and Sissy agree on. I was lucky, real lucky, I never got caught. But luck runs out, that's what Sissy keeps saying.

At the end of his shift, when he gets to sorting the garbage, Woodie decides to take a good look at what's in the trash cans this time. He closes the door of the janitor's office and quickly lifts the lids and puts them on the floor. He empties the trash slowly, tapping the sides, to watch as rosary beads, small plastic toys, a bible, keys, toothpaste, jeans with sequined motifs all tumble into the deep trash cans. Something catches his eye. It's one of the last objects to fall out. It's small. Pointy. It's a hairpin, the colour of pale lemon. He's seen those kind of hairpins on Sissy's dressing table. This one is beaded with tiny butterflies decorating one end and, at the other end, a sharp length of needle that would snake through hair. But that pretty piece isn't garbage, he tells himself. That's one thing I'm sure of, no matter what Raquel says. Before he knows it, Woodie's slipped the hairpin into his pocket. Trash can lids back on.

As he turns to put away his cleaning equipment, the hairpin starts to feel like a lead weight in his pocket. That'll be your conscience. That's why your pocket is feeling so heavy. It's Sissy who's talking to him now, in his head. Listen to your conscience. Do not steal. That's where you went wrong before. And your luck will run out. Sure as eggs is eggs. Remember? Woodie does. And I am, Sissy, listening to my conscience. I am. That's why the hairpin's in my pocket. I just can't throw it away. He hears the door open behind him.

'William Hardwood,' a voice says. 'What's taking your time? Anyone in the trash, hiding away? Immigrants that we've missed?'

Woodie turns around all flushed. First rule of stealing. Act normal, he tells himself.

'Oh, just being tidy. Yes, ma'am.'

'Nice work out there this morning. Good clean floor,' Raquel says. 'Just keep it that way.'

Oh boy, I'm lucky. Still lucky, Woodie says to himself.

Mamá, what happened to el Nica?

Lupita remembers the Nicaraguan boy, the teenager who latched onto them at Chiapas, on the border. He moved up to give her some room on the roof of the train when he saw José appear. El Nica fell off. There was nothing anyone could do. One minute he was there, curled up on the roof of the train. The next, he slid like a sack of corn off the train. A small scraping on metal, his knapsack zipper on the roof, that was the only sound of his body. He must have been fast asleep.

They make the sign of the cross.

Woodie's back home now. He's finished work for the day. He and Sissy are in the kitchen. Sissy has the hairpin in her hand. She turns it over in her palm.

'How'd you get that out?' Sissy asks.

'X-ray on the in. No x-ray on the out.'

Woodie smiles sheepishly. If there's one thing I'm good at, and should get an A-grade for, that's stealing, he says to himself.

'Pretty little thing,' Sissy says. 'It belongs to a woman with long hair. She'll coil her hair around her hand, put in a few twists and turns, and a flick. Then, she'll slide this through and in a shake of a bob cat's tail, her hair's up, the back of her neck's cool.'

She shows him with her own hair.

'Must belong to someone,' she says. 'But that ain't none of your business. Ain't none of my business. Ain't none of our business.' She looks fiercely at Woodie. 'Don't you go back to your old magpie ways, taking anything that catches your fancy.'

But Woodie's already been wondering who the hairpin belongs to. He also tells himself it'll only get him into trouble. Trouble might mean he'll lose his job.

And he's only just got the job. And Sissy's got a doctor's appointment next week. But he's still wondering who the hairpin belongs to before he falls asleep that night.

The following morning, Woodie's made a decision. He knows two wrongs don't make a right. But he also knows what he's decided is more right than wrong. What makes it more right is that he's not keeping what's in the trash cans for himself, like he did in his magpie days. He's keeping the contents for those people locked up in the detention center. What he hasn't figured out is how to return them. He'll work that bit out later.

Woodie takes only what fits in his pockets. He's careful, bringing home a single object in a day. These things are not garbage; they shouldn't go in with uneaten food, with wrappers, with God knows what shit that gets thrown out daily, he tells himself. He knows that for sure. Woodie's mantra is 'keep it small'. He looks around at the people he sees every day as he cleans. This here rosary, is it yours señora Mother Hen? Yours Mrs Bob Cat, or yours señora Wide Ass with the long black plait like a ship's rope down your back? What about you, señorita Deepest Brownest Eyes I've ever seen in this world? And Peanut? Cute Little Peanut who always eats peanuts and makes a mess on my floor. What belongs to you?

Lupita pulls the children close. They huddle under the spindly tree.

Tell me again what Papá's phone number is.

You've asked a million times. I can't keep repeating

it. You know what it is. When we get to the border, Papá said to wait. The coyote will come find us and take us across.

After a month working at the detention center, Raquel isn't there one day when Woodie arrives at the reception area. Frank tells him Raquel's called in sick. No matter. He doesn't need jokes. Doesn't need Raquel to tell him what to do, or to check up on him. He works fast. He also knows it'll be easier to fill his pockets from the trash can without Raquel patrolling around.

Towards the end of his shift, as Woodie cleans the floor of the main communal area, a domino tile spins across the floor. It ricochets off his pail. It's a double six. He watches it fly away. A double blank comes next. It spins off in another direction. Before Woodie can gather the two tiles, a double five arrives. Okay. I'm not that stupid, Woodie says to himself. I know when I'm a target. He looks up.

There's a game of dominoes happening across the way, the tiles rattling on the tabletop, being tapped impatiently as a slow poke thinks about the next move. It's a group of children, their legs under the table, swinging backwards and forwards. Staring straight at him is a boy. The boy holds out a tile towards him. Can I? Can I really play with them? Woodie thinks. No. I can't. I'll lose my job. He hears Sissy's voice. Don't mess up, Woodie. Don't mess up. We need the money. Woodie shakes his head at the boy and carries on cleaning. He's on all fours giving the floor a good scrub. A small pair of feet appear in front of him. The toes curl up and down.

'¿Quieres jugar?' Do you want to play? says the boy to Woodie. 'Por favor.' Please.

Woodie looks around. Raquel's now been signed off sick for the rest of the week. That's what Frank said to him at his break time. Cat's not here, the mice can play. And before he knows it, he starts to move towards the table. Second rule of stealing and all wrongdoing is: don't stand out. He keeps on cleaning as he inches his way to the domino table. The boys are like puppies, hopping on and off their chairs. They just need to get outside and meet a fly or two, Woodie thinks.

The children jabber away. Woodie is now close enough to the table to see what's going on. The boy has sat back down. They all make a sudden sweep, pooling the tiles and counting them out, swiping them from the middle. Woodie spots a pile left to one side. The children wait. They start looking at him. The tiles are for him, Woodie's worked that out. The children say something. Each time they say it, they collapse with laughter. El Flaco. Woodie can tell it's a name for him. Name calling hasn't changed a jot since he was at school. Oh heck, he says to himself. They're waiting for me to start. He quickly plays a domino tile. The children respond in turn. Soon Woodie's running late on his jobs. He stands up by the table. He plays his last tile. He's lost. The tiles are pushed to the center again. The small boy turns to Woodie.

'José,' he says, holding out his hand.

Woodie shakes it.

'Mi hermana,' José says. My sister. He points across

the room. 'Irene.'

The boy rolls the three syllables of her name out slowly as a carpet unfurls. I-re-nee. Three even syllables, like the beginning of a song. Woodie sees a girl across the floor. She's walking with a woman. Her mother, he guesses. The girl notices her brother. They mouth something at each other. José makes some kind of face back. She grins and walks off. Woodie gasps as she turns. Jeez. That ain't puppy fat. How the heck did that happen? How old is she?

The boy repeats the telephone number. He's going to call Papá as soon as he finds a phone. He'll ask to borrow one. And then it'll be alright. Papá will come and get them.

Woodie's telling Sissy about José, the game of dominoes and Irene with the puppy fat that isn't puppy fat. They're in the kitchen eating dinner.

'That's what happens to the women and the young girls,' Sissy says. 'That's the risk they take when they head north. And that ain't part of no one's dream. Now. Don't you get involved. Just don't. It's none of our business. It's bigger than us. It's po-lit-i-cal.' She says the word slowly.

Sissy has already explained the joke to Woodie about the Beast; the same name for the presidential car and the freight trains running through Mexico, loaded with cement, wheat, fertiliser and migrants on the roof. She's said many times Woodie needs to keep up, read the papers and listen to the news. He's living in a dream world if he doesn't know what's been going on, right on their doorstep for decades.

'Get with the times, bro. Wake up!' she says. 'We've all got our problems. What do you want? One of them coming and taking your job?'

Woodie stands up and scrapes his chair back across the kitchen floor.

'Where you going?' Sissy asks. 'You're all jackrabbity tonight.'

Woodie doesn't answer.

'What you up to?' Sissy says. 'I can tell from that look on your face.'

Woodie's halfway up the stairs. Ever since he discovered Saint Oscar Romero, he's been doing his own research. It's been hard to do it in secret. He's never been good at keeping secrets, what with a sister like Sissy. And he has been keeping up with the news and with the times. Sissy's wrong there. He knows what's going on. There are going to be more border patrols starting in the next few days. More helicopters, more ground searches, more dogs. He's been following the news and emailing people, those humanitarian organisations to find out what's really happening. It doesn't feel political. It feels personal, everyday personal, right-under-his-nose personal. Woodie runs up the stairs. He knows he has to go tonight, or he might get caught with more patrols coming.

An hour later, Woodie tip toes to the front door. He's holding his boots, his knapsack strapped on. The car's all packed.

'Where you going? It's late to be going out,' Sissy

says from the kitchen.

'Tell you later,' Woodie says.

Woodie slips out the house. He opens the trunk of his car. It's full to the brim with water bottles. He's been collecting them from the trash for weeks. All different sizes, from small to medium, and then to larger gallon sized ones. He's filled them up with water and stowed them in the car. He closes the trunk and jumps in. He's got tingling in his hands. He tells himself that he needs to do something. He can't just scrub those floors, come home and sit and scratch his skinny backside and do nothing. Woodie talks to himself as he checks the map he's got out on his lap. He's made a big X at a major crossing point, deep in the Sonoran Desert, towards Sasabe and the border.

Woodie drives quickly. He'll only be able to do short trips, radiating out from where he parks the car. He has to do it all tonight. He's checked the directions and map a hundred times. He spots the turn off. Parks and opens up the trunk and walks with the small water bottles first, launching them as far as he can in different directions. It's dark. He hears the bottles land in the sand. He then takes the medium-sized ones and does the same, throwing them in a new direction. The big ones, he just lifts them out the trunk and places them beside the car. He picks up the last bottle, reads the message, same as he's written on each one.

As he drives home, Woodie turns on the radio and finds some music to listen to. He smiles, remembering what the children called him earlier. He laughed right out when Sissy told him what it meant. El Flaco. The

159

skinny one. As Woodie rolls down the window, the wind blows through his hair. He thinks back to how he had to drop the water off in the dark, without a flashlight, without any light. He suddenly realises that he isn't afraid of the dark anymore. He shouts out into the desert, I am El Flaco. El Flaco. In the still of the night, in the big pitch-black expanse of the Sonoran Desert, his voice echoes back.

The Blackhawk helicopter hovers overhead. Searchlights slice through the darkness. SUVs head for the targeted area behind the rocks.

I see 'em. Hold the dog back! This is the US Border Patrol. I repeat. Put your hands up. Okay. I see two juveniles and a woman.

Grab that boy and kick those fuckin' water bottles til they burst, will you?

It's been three days since he went on his night expedition. Woodie puts his key in the lock. As he opens the door, he hears Sissy calling out to him. Her voice comes speeding down the hallway.

'Shut the front door. You come right away into the kitchen and explain yourself.'

Woodie catches himself in the mirror. He's got that look on his face. Maybe his luck's running out. He hangs up his jacket and walks into the kitchen.

'Goddamn it, Woodie. Can't you just go to work and come home without talking to the whole of Arizona, like you're on your own public address system?' Sissy says. 'They'll recognise your dumb way of speaking. And then they'll fire you for saying what you did.' Her hand's on the radio. She's turning up the volume. 'Listen up.'

Woodie hears his voice coming through the speaker. Why did you do it? Shooting your mouth off like some snake oil seller of a politician, he says to himself. Just got too overconfident since the water drop. Couldn't help pulling the car over and calling in to the radio talk show. Woodie can hear himself, loud and clear, his words hanging in the air in the kitchen. *They're just unlucky. They want a better life. Una vida mejor. Yup. That's all. Una vida mejor.* That's him, the janitor, booming around the kitchen talking about the illegal migrants.

Well, Arizona county, the calls are coming in thick and fast. It's like a stampede now. Let's take the next caller to respond to one of our earlier callers, Tucker Quinn.

'It's been on repeat all morning.' Sissy raises an eyebrow. 'Tucker Quinn? Why on earth did you have to use Grandpa's name?'

Woodie's still standing at the kitchen door.

'Sit down, Woodie. Just sit down,' Sissy says, dragging a chair out for him.

Caller, give us your name first and then let's hear what you have to say, the phone-in host says.

Well, hello y'all. I'm Carter, Carter Johnson Jr, a man with a deep dark voice that sounds as if it comes from the bottom of a barrel says. *All I want to say to Tucker Quinn,* the man says, *is you don't know jack shit.*

Woodie's heart speeds up.

We need to close the border down because we've had enough of them. Who the hell do they think they are, thinking they can pack up their families and their goddamn children and drag them through hell to get to our border? Your border! My border!

In the car, as soon as he'd hung up, Woodie had turned the radio off. He'd headed home, only making a detour to buy a lottery ticket for Sissy, like he always does. Sissy clicks her finger at him to get his attention.

'There's more,' she says. 'He hasn't finished. Listen up.'

We don't want transnational criminals here. We don't want their gangs. We don't want their drugs. Our presidents, none of them, want them here. We don't want them here. I don't want them here. Period!

There's a pause.

Tucker Quinn. I hope you're listening to me. Because I want you and the rest of Arizona to hear what I'm about to say.

Woodie's sitting up ramrod straight, now staring ahead. He nods his head to Carter Johnson Jr's instructions. He wipes his face as if the spittle, that he's sure the man is emitting, is hitting him fair and square in the face. He can feel it, sliding down his cheeks, his chin.

Sissy turns the radio off.

'Well, brother. You just flushed out a whole lotta hate, all by your skinny self, without even thinking of the consequences for us. People find out it was you, we'll soon be getting hate mail. Dog turds in our mailbox,' she says. 'Or worse.'

Woodie stands. His legs feel unsteady. He holds the table with one hand. He puts his other hand in his pocket, drops the Mega Millions lottery ticket on the table, and walks out.

The boy repeats the number. I'll call Papá. Then he'll come. He'll come and fetch us like Mamá said.

Woodie has a loop going in his head ever since the phone-in. He shouts as he drives to work the next day. He's got a lot to say to Carter Johnson Jr. When he checks through Security, Raquel's already standing in reception. She's back. He doesn't care if someone's told her about the game of dominoes. The third rule of stealing is, always expect to be caught. Woodie goes straight to the janitor's office. He puts on his overalls. As he turns, he sees Raquel standing there.

'What you got to say to me, William Hardwood?' Raquel says.

Before the phone-in, he would have played for time. But not today. Woodie doesn't say anything. He begins filling up his pail, starts checking his cloths are all ready to go, cleaning trolly, his sleeves rolled up.

'All talked out?' Raquel says. 'Well, I've something to say.'

Woodies waits. He knows he's trapped.

'It's funny when you're sick in bed, with a fever, thinking that no one loves you, that the world is full of sickos, and the sickos are just full of anger and hate, and we're all going to hell 'cos that's what we all deserve for the shit we're in today. Then, out of nowhere, you hear this voice. You're not sure if you're dreamin' cos you have a fever.'

Woodie doesn't know what in cat's hell Raquel is talking about.

'You crack me up, William Hardwood,' Raquel says, slapping Woodie across the back. 'I'll get to my point. Well, I never, ever, listen to the radio. Never like all that hill billy country music. And I never listen to phone-ins. But I did this week 'cos I was feeling right sorry for myself. Anyways, I kept hearing this voice. I kept thinking I know that person who repeats himself when he gets nervous. Who speaks real slow and spits out what he wants to say one word at a time. And pretends he's real dumb.'

Woodie knows the most important rule of stealing is to say nothing and keep moving. Be quick but not too quick. He heads to the door.

'You know what, Tucker Quinn…' Raquel says.

Woodie stops in his tracks. He turns slowly to face Raquel.

'You pay no attention to that lowdown rattlesnake, Carter-I'll-see-you-in-hell-Johnson Jr. Don't ever stop expressing your own opinion, Woodie, in your state, in your country. It's your democratic right. You are a good American. But,' and she pauses, 'don't ever do that on my watch again, do you hear me?'

Woodie nods.

'And no playing dominoes with those kids. You're only here to clean.'

Raquel walks out ofhe janitor's room, closing the door behind her. Now he knows his luck hasn't run out.

Not yet. He knows he can't make José or Irene or anyone's dreams come true. But he's just going to say this one thing, the same as what he wrote on every single bottle of water he dropped in the desert. He's been rehearsing what he's going to say to Irene. Que tengas suerte. May you be lucky. He's decided to give Irene the pale lemon hairpin. It's the only thing he can do as life is complicada.

Jacaranda tree

I

As he checks the surf, Ray takes a quick look up at the cliffs. Before he's even picked up his board and walked down to the beach, before he's even set foot in the water, he's thinking about her. It's become a habit. The young woman is there today. He can see her from his position on the beach. She's like a figurehead on a boat, looking out to sea. Always at Black Dog Point. It's been going on for weeks now. He knows when she's there and when she isn't.

Stepping into the water with his board, Ray watches and waits to see what the waves are doing. He finds a spot out the back. He paddles towards it. No one else is out on the water. It's a sign the weather front is coming in. He sits astride his board, rocking with the swell as it heaves and rolls. He looks back towards the beach. With the onshore southerly, he won't have long. I'll just give it a few and see what happens. He picks a wave.

Nothing. Ray paddles out again. Last time, he says to himself. Final wave home. He glances up to the cliffs again. Still there. It's not his lookout if something happens when the weather front hits the cliffs. Old enough and big enough to look after herself. Yeah. Not his fault. He's sure of that. Well, maybe.

A thought comes to him. Ray tries to dismiss it. It keeps coming back. There was a jumper last week. Jim, his new neighbour, had mentioned it when he was helping Ray with his car at the weekend. He glances again up at the cliffs to the young woman. He's thinking. Usually if there's an incident, it's a stupid inexperienced surfer getting pushed onto the rocks. Or a swimmer caught in a good old South Sydney rip and copping it. Next stop the Southern Ocean via the Pacific or Tassie.

The weather's changing fast. Ray decides to pack it in and get out of the water. He lies on his board and heads towards the beach, riding the slow, lumbering arching swell. Before he reaches the sand, he knows he'll take the route home along the cliff path, past where the young woman is sitting. As he walks off the beach, he's thinking about what he's going to say to her. Christ Ray, you're an idiot, thinking you can just talk to a stranger sitting on a cliff edge. You're the last person she'll want to see. Well, that's a good thing then.

Up on the cliff, Cathy turns her face out to sea, to the weather front coming directly in through the heads of the bay. Stormy weather, no better time to be out here, she thinks. It's difficult to pick out the horizon in the fading light. The darkening clouds are backlit by the setting sun. She looks down beyond her feet to the bottom of the cliff. The drag of the sea is growing, the undertow sucking back the water from the headland and the beach. The sea's churning. The beach is deserted, except for the lone surfer. Ah, she sees him paddling in now. Idiot, going out in this weather.

She sits in the hard sandstone seat, worn and shaped by the salt-laden wind and looks up to the rising moon, as if the invisible pull that brings in the water will reveal itself to her. She imagines a thin thread of gossamer, tugging on the water below. It makes her think of Aunty Wilma. Aunty Wilma loved the sea, loved coming to sit in this very spot. Sit outside with the sky and the wind, and it'll be right, Aunty Wilma would always say to Cathy. The wind bickers above. The sea roars below. It's like an argument without winners. But Cathy senses she isn't alone on the cliff. She's heard a voice above the waves and the wind.

'Hey! Hey!' the voice calls again.

It's a man's voice. Nick off. There's no way I'm going to talk to you, she says to herself. If I ignore him, he'll probably shove off. She's sick of blokes coming on to her thinking she's fair game. She turns to see who it is. It's the surfer. She just saw him paddle back onto the beach. She watched him get out and shake his head like a dog trying to dry itself. He must have come straight off the beach and walked up the path. Doesn't usually come this way. He has his wet suit rolled down, longboard under his arm.

'Have you got the time?' Ray says.

He's dripping with sea water and shivering, half a

grin on his face.

Cathy doesn't reply.

'So, are you going to answer my question?' Ray says.

She waves her bare wrists at him.

'Nope,' she says

'Are you going to keep sitting there?' Ray says.

Ray's teeth are chattering. The wind whips up Cathy's hair. She's not a jumper, that's for sure, he decides. What was he thinking? But he's got to do something now that he's standing there like a lemon. Ray puts his board down. Takes off his watch.

'Meet me at the beach tomorrow arvo?' Ray says, holding out his watch. 'Near the Jacaranda trees. Four o' clock?'

Cathy gets up from her cliff edge seat and walks across. She takes it from him. That's pretty cheeky, she thinks.

'See you tomorrow then,' he says. 'And keep away from cliff edges. Storm's coming in.'

'You don't need to tell me that,' she says.

'I'm Ray by the way.'

'Cathy.'

Ray picks up his board. It'll be a story for Jim later.

That evening, Cathy's in the pub telling her sister Leanne about Ray.

'Hooley dooley! He thought, what? Nah! I don't believe it,' Leanne says. She hoots and rocks backwards and forwards on her bar stool. 'He thought you were a jumper on the cliff?'

The question trails off like cigarette smoke circling

up to the roof of the pub.

'You know how it is. It was just me sitting there in the dark, the storm coming in. Usual stuff. I'd finished work and didn't want to be at the house.'

Aunty Wilma had only passed a few months back. She'd been like a mother to Cathy. To them both.

'It's kind of romantic, don't you think? You've got to give him that. The storm, dusk, giving you his watch.' Leanne's eyes are on Cathy's wrist and the watch. 'Must be worth a bit. You know. That brand. Looks silver-plated to me.'

Cathy holds out her arm. The watch is too big for her. It slips down over her wrist. No, she doesn't believe in any of that fairy-tale rubbish, pushed on to women. Is that what the watch was all about? I'll give it back to Ray tomorrow, she says to herself.

The next day, the beach is deserted. The weather front has arrived. The wind is up. The swell's high. Sounds of the waves crashing allow Ray and Cathy time to settle, without having to make small talk. They sit on the cold sand, at the high-tide mark, just down from the Jacaranda trees.

'The waves, they're no good. Need a bit of a wind change to clean it all up,' Ray says. 'Once the weather clears, we should get a few good barrels.'

Cathy knows. She's been watching the sea for as long as she can remember. She likes Ray for starting the conversation, for going first. They sit in silence. It seems like a long time to Ray. He's waiting for Cathy to say something.

'It's the oldest sound in the world,' Cathy says, finally.

Ray turns to look at her.

'The sea,' she says.

The sea. Ah, he gets it. She's so right.

Cathy glances at Ray. She can't tell what he's thinking. Sink or swim, she says to herself. He's going to have to take me as he finds me. It's been on her mind for a while now. Every day she catches herself listening for Aunty Wilma, her footsteps, the slam of the door, her breathing, her heavy laugh. She hears her sometimes. She really does. She's never talked to anyone before about this, not even to Leanne.

'Have you ever heard them?' she says.

Since Aunty Wilma passed, she's believing more and more in spirits. They must be everywhere around them.

'Just because someone's dead, doesn't mean they go away forever,' Cathy says.

Ah, Ray gets it now. He's worked out what Cathy's talking about. He watches Cathy put her hand on her heart.

'Listen,' she says again. 'You've got to be still. And listen here too.' She pats her heart. 'If you're still, they'll come.'

And maybe Aunty Wilma will. It was something about the weather yesterday. As if the wind had brought him in off the water, off the beach and up the path. To her. Aunty Wilma behind him. She couldn't explain it any other way. Cathy catches Ray's eye.

'Stuff that's true isn't always written in books. That's what my Aunty Wilma always says.'

Ray looks at Cathy's wrist. He notices she's still wearing his watch.

II

It's early morning. The house is quiet. Ben and Skye are at a sleepover at Leanne's, the last one before Leanne and Geoff move south. There are bikes and skateboards in the hallway, shoes and coats on the floor, washing up in the sink. The Jacaranda tree's back. It's made its entrance again. Always in October. The frothy sway of blue and purple flowers bends heavily on the charcoal branches. Cathy stops writing to look at the tree through the window.

Why did I do it? It didn't mean anything. It was one night. Why didn't I just talk to Ray first and say I was unhappy. He'd just appeared at the sea pool one evening and dived underneath her. In her lane. She could see his spine and shoulder blades as he powered beneath her, like a dolphin, all muscle and compact.

'Pick your stroke and I'll race you,' he said, when he came up for air and they were both at the same end of the swim lane. 'See who wins.'

She won. And Leanne bollocked her. Ray didn't. Leanne called her stupid, an idiot. Messing a good bloke around. She meant Ray. Ray didn't ask for the sordid details. Leanne did. He only wanted to know what he hadn't been able to give her. Cathy didn't know.

She still doesn't know. Cathy shuts down this image of Ray in her head and goes back to looking at the Jacaranda tree through the window. Its branches hover over the yard. She glances at her watch knowing Ray will be up soon. The last conversation that she and Ray had is going round and around in her head.

'I thought when we met,' Ray had said, 'that it would be forever. We would be forever.'

Forever! The word had ricocheted around the lounge. Forever, a word from fairy tales, a word from the playground. I'll be your friend forever. Look forever young, the adverts scream. The couple who say they'll love each other forever. And what did Leanne say the other night? The thing is, Cathy. Life just isn't a bed of roses. We all know that. Well, we're all supposed to know that. You've got Skye and Ben now. Responsibilities.

Cathy hears Leanne's voice, life just isn't a bed of roses, life just isn't a bed of roses. She shakes her head. Avoiding reality. Isn't that what Ray said last night? You just aren't facing up to what's happening here! And he had underlined the word *here* with a raised voice.

In their bedroom, Ray wakes up. For a split second, his mind is elsewhere, in a quiet calm spot, and now it's snatched back. He groans. A small sound escapes from his mouth. He turns over and curls up, as he remembers the night before. He opens his eyes. The space beside him is empty, the sheet still holding the indent of her shape. He should go to work. He notices his throat is sore. Ah, I remember that now. Shouldn't have shouted. It just came from nowhere. Shout and it's all over. Ray gets up. He goes to the kitchen.

Cathy hears a mug placed on the table, a kettle switched on, the fridge door pulled open and then shut. She sits listening. The kettle clicks off. She hears water poured into the mug. She counts the seconds. She knows how long Ray likes his tea to brew. The fridge door opens again. Then footsteps. Ray walks into the lounge. He looks in her direction and forms the letter T with his fingers. She nods back. He leaves. She hears the routine all over again. The mug on the kitchen table, the kettle goes on, the fridge opens and shuts. The kettle clicks off. She counts. He knows she likes her tea a bit stronger. He comes back with two mugs and passes her one.

'Ta,' Cathy says.

They sit in silence.

'Have you noticed the Jacaranda?' Cathy finally asks.

It's unlike her to start a conversation, Ray thinks. He listens to her telling the Jacaranda story, how the tree came from Brazil. It's as if she's forgotten that she's already told him it before. Many times. He lets the words lap around him, like the sea around his ankles. He's exhausted by words and their inadequacy. There must be a way of sorting this out. He finishes his tea. Cathy's still talking. She's now telling her favourite childhood story, about Aunty Wilma's teeth. Cathy's imitating Aunty Wilma. He listens to the long stretched out syllables of her words, and the way her tone moves like a swing seat, high to low, low to high.

'I can get by without them! No need for those fellas poking around my gob, like looking under a car bonnet.'

Ray treasures the comfort of the story. After all, it was Aunty Wilma who brought them together. Well, that's what they both like to believe. Who else would have made Ray go up to the cliff that night with the weather front coming in? Why else would Cathy have agreed to meet Ray on the beach? But what's driving them apart? The Big Drift, he calls it. He's noticed for some time that Cathy's lost her feistiness. It's what he's always liked about her, not being part of the herd, different, a standing out from the crowd sort of person. Now she seems less.

Ray watches the Jacaranda tree through the window. He looks at the heavy pendant-like flowers, the lime-green ferny leaves. It's been there for as long as he's known Cathy. Even longer. The flowers keep coming back every spring. Out of the corner of his eye, he notices she's looking at it too.

'What I find strange,' Cathy says, 'is that from these beautiful purply blue flowers, as soon as they drop on the ground, they turn to a brown sludgy mess.'

Ray thinks Cathy might say something more. He waits. But she doesn't. He shifts in his chair. They're not talking about what they need to talk about. We've got to stop banging on about the Jacaranda tree, he says to himself. He glances at her. Do you want me? Or shall we just pack it all in and tell Ben and Skye that we're over and out? It's still a question. And as long as it's still a question, Ray knows there's hope they might work something out.

They sit there. Cathy takes a quick look at Ray. She catches his eye. They both look away. The sound of a kookaburra in the Jacaranda tree fills the room. Ray gets up and goes to the kitchen to make another cuppa. What did Jim say? He thinks of last night when he and Jim had a quick surf. They were talking about women and love. About Cathy. And the swimmer. The Fucking Pool Swimmer, as Ray calls him.

'Have you tried to talk to her? Really talk to her?' Jim had said. 'It takes two to tango, you know. Most of us blokes can't do that difficult stuff. One sniff of it and we're off like a bride's nightie.'

Jim's words had made him think. The kettle clicks off. Ray pours the hot water. Maybe that's the point. The whole point. Maybe, I'm not like most blokes. I'm not going to bail out. He glances back towards the lounge. He can't see Cathy. He stops what he's doing and goes to check. She isn't there. Her chair's empty, her watch lying on the arm. He goes back down the corridor to the bedrooms, the kids' rooms and then theirs. The bathroom door is open. He looks through the house. She's nowhere to be seen. Her shoes are still there. He knows she hasn't gone to work. She's not teaching until the afternoon.

Ray's heart sinks. He'd thought there was hope. That they could talk it through. That they would work it out. The car's in the driveway. The fly screen door is closed. She must have shut it carefully so he wouldn't hear it slam in its usual way. Ray leaves the house. He's still in his boxers. Where would she have gone? Up to the Oval? No. Not without the kids. He runs barefoot towards the beach. She can only be there. Mad thoughts rush through his head. He hadn't meant to lean on her so much last night. He just wanted to be sure, to be sure about them, if there was still a chance.

The beach is ahead. He sees the wide expanse of ocean, sun sparkling and dancing on its surface. He checks the cliffs. He scans the beach. Spots a single set of footprints. That's all he needs. It doesn't take him long to catch sight of Cathy, sitting above the tide mark. Ray jumps straight onto the sand, feeling the cold beneath his feet. He stands still for a moment, waiting. He watches her to see if she might move. The last thing he wants to do is to spook her. When he thinks she's settled, he walks towards her. She doesn't look up at him. But he notices she makes the smallest of movements, opening up the tiniest of spaces for him to slip into. It's a welcome, Cathy style. Ray sits. He sees a Jacaranda flower in front of her, its purply blue petals dusted with grains of sand.

'Found it lying in the road,' Cathy says. 'Couldn't just leave it there.'

They sit a while, knees brushing, watching the surf roll in, small curling pipes of crystal-clear green water. They watch how the sea slackens as it comes up the beach, how it turns slowly into elliptical bends and curves.

'I'm waiting,' she says. 'Aunty Wilma might come. I haven't spoken to her for a while.'

Ray nods. He understands. They sit together listening to the sea roll in.

'You know what Aunty Wilma always says?' Cathy asks.

He waits.

'She says, don't spend too long walking in the soft sand.'

Spot on, Aunty Wilma, Ray says to himself. He reaches in his pocket and takes out his watch. He gives it to her.

III

Ben can taste the smoke. The air outside his parents' house is thick with it. It's acrid. Bitter. Up above, it's a dirty-orange colour. No one's slept properly for weeks. There's been a creeping anxiety, fuelled by national news, pictures from space and the gut-affirming reality that the bush fires are far worse than they have ever been. On the news, climate scientists say, we warned you. But no one listened. Aboriginal elders say, no one ever listens to us. We must live with the land. Not live off it. The land is our mother. The fire services say they're at breaking point. We told you months ago this would happen. You, meaning the government.

The fires started way before the official bushfire season. Ben knows his mother always rolls her eyes at that expression. There's nothing official about fire, she says. It's ancient, spiritual, sacred, but official? Nope. These fires have been raging for months. They're ferocious. Out of control. Millions of hectares burning. Areas the size of the UK, Portugal, the news says.

Ben opens his phone and replays the video Skye sent

him. He's noticed his sister has got angrier the longer she's been helping out with the wildlife rescue. The fires have been devastating, the number of animals incinerated unimaginable. He watches the video for the umpteenth time. Skye looks exhausted, streaked with sweat, smoke and charcoal.

'Benno, look at this! It's just mind blowing.'

The camera pans around the burnt bushland. 'It's hell on earth.'

'We just picked this little fella up,' she says, and she holds up a koala, its feet wrapped in pink bandages.

And now, their parents have gone missing. He and Skye decided they'd gone officially missing two days ago. On New Year's Day. They hatched a plan quickly. Skye to stay down the coast exactly where she is, Ben to travel to their parents' home to wait it out. Ben still can't understand why his parents decided to go south. Just before Christmas, they said they were off to see Aunty Leanne and Uncle Geoff. No, of course they weren't going to go anywhere near the fires. They weren't stupid.

But then the fires spread, coming up from the south from Mallacoota, then east from Cobargo, and down from the national parks near Nowra. And by New Year's Eve there were fires all along the South Coast, right where their parents had said they were heading. Cities and towns had become engulfed in the haze. Fire alarms triggered, smoke alarms too. The ferries in Sydney Harbour honked their fog horns.

Ben glances through the window to the Jacaranda tree in the backyard. He sees its leaves with a sheer covering of ash, dulling the natural lime-green. He tries his parents' mobile phones again. He dials his mother's, gets her voicemail. He hears her youthful sing-song voice. She'll call him back when she can, she promises. Then he calls his father's. He can't leave a message. Ray's voicemail is full. Ben knows the fires are destroying the mobile phone towers; power lines are coming down and the Fires Near Me app isn't working properly because the fires are moving too fast. Come on, Skye, call! Call me, Ben says to himself.

The hardest thing is to do nothing. No. The hardest thing is to wait. To wait in the absence of information. He's been checking hourly the website of the Evacuation Centre at Ulladulla. From the television and radio, he knows that the fire services are beat—beat by the heat, by the lack of sleep, by the sheer size, pace, ferocity of the fires, by exploding eucalypts and their natural oil fuelling the fire. Like kerosene. Fires move way faster than a person can run, he knows that. And, as Skye says all the time, faster than a koala because koalas can't run. They're tree dwellers. Kangaroos and wallabies can run if they can get over the fences. Otherwise, they're trapped like everybody and everything else. Nope, Ben tells himself. He's not going to think about that right now.

In his parents' kitchen, he looks around. It's as if they've only just got up. He sees their cups by the kettle. There's no point looking at those all day, he says to himself. He'll go to the beach. As he steps onto the front porch, he waves to Jim, their neighbour from way back. Jim waves and leaves it at that. Jim knows. Everyone knows why Ben is here. The air is thick and hazy. The beach, when it comes into view, is a shocker. It's black with ash, millions and millions of ash particles sent by the wind, from the raging fires up north. Ben watches how the sea brings in the ash, wave by wave, depositing it in long swathes of curling black ribbon along the sand, creating a boundary between him and the water.

All their lives, they've watched what comes in off the ocean. And it's never been like this. It's no place to sit, Ben decides. He heads back towards the house. Jim's still there, outside with the clippers now. Funny thing to be pruning, on a day like this. Doing the everyday things, to make it all feel better. Normal. This time he walks up to Jim. They slap each other awkwardly around the shoulders.

'How you doing, Benno?'

'Waiting.'

'Yup, that's all you can do. Come over if you fancy some company. We're not talkers, as you know, me and Jean. Just come. And sit. Have a cuppa.'

Jim and Jean, they've always been part of his life. Him and Skye used to disappear from their house and appear in Jim and Jean's when the rows got too bad. Jean always said, door's never locked, everyone knows that, even the burglars. Come in and make yourself toast with vegemite. Put the telly on. And they did. Often. Melting from one house to the other. Until everything had quietened down between their parents. Funny to think back to all that. Another time. Another life. But still the same people. Good people, Jim and Jean would say about his parents. The best, his parents would say about their neighbours and life-long friends.

Ben heads back into the house. He realises he still doesn't know if Skye has managed to get hold of Aunty Leanne and Uncle Geoff. He decides to give it a try himself. He dials. There's no connection. He dials again. He hears ringing. A voice. He's got through. He'd better be quick.

'Aunty Leanne?' he says. 'Aunty Leanne, it's Ben.'

'I know, darlin'. I know it's you. So good to hear you.' There's silence.

'Are you alright, Aunty Leanne? And Uncle Geoff?'

'Yes, darlin'. We're right. Just. The fire was coming through. They said we had to leave.'

Ben knows how it works. You have your bags packed, all ready, and once you're told to leave, you leave immediately. No hanging around, not for a minute longer, and you follow the evacuation routes. He can hardly hear Aunty Leanne. Her voice is raspy. The line fluctuates.

'I said to Mum and Dad, to come when I'm out of hospital. No point coming now. It's a good thing I put them off,' she says.

Hospital? His parents hadn't said anything to him about Aunty Leanne being sick. It isn't how his mum had told it to Ben and Skye. So, me and Dad, we're going to surprise Leanne and Geoff. Just turn up. With the beers and an esky full of food. Just surprise them. They'll love that. It'll be like old times, having a good yarn together.

'Good thing, they never came,' Aunty Leanne says. 'Now, don't you go worrying about me, Benno. I'll be right. I will be. No need to be a worry wart like your mum. You know what she can be like.'

Before Ben can say anything, the line goes dead. So that's why his parents had suddenly decided to go down the coast. To be with Aunty Leanne when she has her operation. Did Mum listen to Aunty Leanne? Knowing her, she probably ignored Aunty Leanne's advice to come later. I'm not going to think about the fact they never made it to Aunty Leanne's, Ben says to himself. Just going to ignore it. Not going to think about it.

Ben has the fidgets as he walks around the house. He goes into his parents' bedroom. Picks up an old photo, the one of his parents on the longboard. Dad at the back, Mum at the front with the wind in her face. He spots the paperweight Dad had made with the Jacaranda blossom. He said it was the most romantic thing he had ever done. It was. It is. No one was allowed to touch the paperweight. No one is allowed to touch it. But Ben picks it up and puts it in his pocket. He decides to go up to the cliffs. As he leaves the house, he sends Skye a message telling her that he's spoken to Aunty Leanne.

Jogging up to the cliffs, Ben thinks back to the story of how his parents met, how his mum was watching his dad out on his board and thought he was an idiot to be surfing in such bad weather. How his dad saw his mum up on those very cliffs, and thought she was a jumper. A jumper! They would laugh away, catching each other's eyes through the tears of laughter. They both agreed it was all Aunty Wilma's doing. That's who Ben needs to be with. Aunty Wilma. She's always there. Sit outside with the sky and the wind and it'll be right.

At the top of the cliff, Ben sees fencing. The council's been and blocked off the top. He can't sit in the weathered seat, right at the edge. He stands on the path. It's calm and breezeless, even this high up. He looks down to the sea. In it comes, foaming, frothing, climbing up the cliff, only to recede back out. As he watches, Ben feels a small sense of calm return, a calm he normally only feels when he's out in the water with his sister on the boards, waiting for the last wave of the day to bring them in to the beach.

Above the sound of the water, he hears a voice.

'Cooee!'

He ignores it. He wants to be alone. But, then again, he doesn't. He turns. It's Jim. He must have been hard on his heels. Jim stands there, his hand raised. He says something. Ben can't make out what. He gets up and walks towards him.

'Alright Benno?'

'Yeah, just listening to the sea.'

Jim slips his arm around his shoulder.

'Oldest sound in the world,' Jim says. 'Skye called. Said she couldn't get you.'

Ben looks at his phone. There's a missed call. He doesn't recognise the number. 'What did she say?' He searches Jim's face for bad news.

'She didn't. Just said she'd left you a message. She managed to borrow a satellite phone,' Jim says. 'All the lines are down now.'

Ben and Jim walk back down the path, while Ben listens to Skye's message. He gives Jim the thumbs ups.

'They're safe,' he says. 'She couldn't talk for long. They were on the beach. Mum and Dad made it to the beach.'

'It's the safest place to be. By the water,' Jim says. 'Thought they'd head there.'

They look out towards the sea. Jim points to a couple of surfers.

'Now, what would your dad say?' Jim says.

'Next stop the Southern Ocean via the Pacific or Tassie.'

It's what they always said as kids, him and Skye. A warning. And a ritual. They watch the surfers for a few minutes.

'I think they know what they're doing. They're good. They'll make it back in,' Ben says.

As they start walking together back down the cliff towards the beach, Ben feels the paperweight in his pocket. It's tapping against his leg. He'll put it back as soon as he's in the house. The wind's picking up. It pushes him from behind.

Alright, Aunty Wilma. Alright, Ben says to himself.

Busy being free

The afternoon Cape Town sun streams in, bathing the 'sorry for being late' flowers in the vase. The heady scent of white lilies hangs in the air. Through the living room window, Thandi looks at the brightly coloured houses of Bo-Kaap. Mauve, red and yellow. She pushes a thought to the back of her mind. It's been there for months, lurking. No, she won't say anything. Not her business even though she's one of Evie's best friends. It's not for her to tell Evie who she should or shouldn't marry.

Thandi sits back on the blue velvet sofa. Across the room, Evie's rocking gently in the rattan chair. She's begun a random story to explain why she's so late for lunch. Something about meeting a man. It sounds like she's started in the middle of the story, which is typical of Evie. Thandi watches Evie stand, walk to her bag and pull out a vinyl record. She pictures Evie's extensive record collection. It fills a complete wall of her living room, together with the Technics turntable and speakers positioned with pinpoint accuracy. Nothing off about Evie's taste in music. Only her timekeeping.

Thandi tells herself to stop harping on about Evie being late. She's always late. Born late. Evie Time is nothing new. Evie waves the psychedelic mustard yellow cover at her. Thandi recognises it immediately. *Song to a Seagull*. It's their favourite Joni Mitchell record. When they shared an apartment, they played it all the time as well as Whitney, Queen Bey, Lizzo and Taylor for break ups. The soundtrack of their twenties.

'Okay, Evie, Let's double back to the beginning. You're on Kloof Street. You happen to be passing Mabu's record store and you go in?' Thandi says.

Their disjointed conversation and Evie's half-finished sentences are frustrating Thandi. No one has eaten yet despite Thandi making their favourite food. And she's still got lots to do for the women's protest march set for next Saturday. Nadine's coming to collect everything for the print shop at five o'clock. Has Evie even remembered? Thandi checks the time. It's already past three. She's trying to piece together the story quickly, following the breadcrumbs through the deep forest of Evie's mind. She knows from long experience that they're nowhere near the beginning.

'No, Thandi. It wasn't like that. I was always heading to the record store. I needed to go there because of this,' Evie says, waving the Joni Mitchell record again and putting it on the coffee table in front of Thandi. 'But okay. I did get side-tracked in Jazz. And he came out of nowhere. He was just there,' Evie says, walking back to the rattan chair. 'In the Jazz section.'

In the Jazz section? Thandi says to herself. She hates

jazz. It's like chicken. It's all the same.

'Evie, your story's sounding like a rom com.' Thandi spots a harsh critical tone creeping into her voice. It's not like her, not like them to be critical of each other. Honest yes. Critical no. 'Sorry, Evie. Forget I just said that. I'm listening. I really am.' She makes herself comfortable on the sofa. This could take a while.

She hasn't seen Evie for a few weeks. Three and a half to be exact. For some reason or other, each had cancelled and then they'd rearranged. And cancelled again. Messaging backwards and forwards instead of talking. A year ago, it would have been unthinkable if Thandi didn't know what Evie was doing on an almost hourly basis. What each other was eating for lunch, what they were both wearing. There's been a shift, a change of direction in their friendship. Thandi's noticed it. Everyone says, oh that's what happens in your thirties. Priorities change. Well, do they? All she knows is that she has an Evie shaped hole in her life.

The turning point in their friendship was when Evie started to say 'we have plans', meaning her and René. It used to be her and Evie, in their late twenties, making plans. Bar hopping Friday nights. The freewheeling weekends when they would decide on the spur of the moment what to do and where to go. Evie's favourite beach at Clifton, lunch with friends, clubbing at the Waterfront, a trip to the vineyards, the Sunday nights in PJs watching a box set, writing their manifesting diaries together. They didn't need a calendar to meet up. Now they do. They also used to talk about their future plans, of travelling, living in Paris. They could be digital nomads. But we never made it to Paris, Thandi says to herself.

Thandi thinks about Evie's boyfriend. No, Evie's fiancé. She feels guilty. When Evie described him as the man of her dreams, Thandi said she'd better get bigger dreams. Well, she was very drunk at the time. René, the kind of man to guide a woman with a hand in the small of her back; to think a group of women are on their own if they aren't with a man. Just a bit bleh. And *that* dinner, Thandi thinks. When she and Julius had met up with Evie and René. Awkward didn't begin to describe it. A short evening. Eating as fast as they could to get out of there. And drinking way too much. Her and Evie. Neither had mentioned it since.

Of course, I feel happy for Evie. I do. Mostly. Well, I try to, Thandi says to herself when the thought of talking to Evie about her impending marriage comes up. But Evie's story about the record store doesn't make sense, about this man, when she's supposed to be getting married to René.

'Okay, my beautiful friend,' Thandi says, 'let's just rewind the tape a bit. You're in Mabu's record store, minding your own business, buying *another* copy of our favourite record. And suddenly this man, this much younger man, has fallen at your feet? Literally?'

Thandi glances at her laptop across the room, with all the papers and stacks of t-shirts she's ordered. She feels an itch to get going on the preparations for the protest. Not talk about the wedding. She flip flops from no, she's not going to talk about it to yes, she's going to bring it up now that Evie is here. In front of her. But

189

how to bring it up without sounding? What? Jealous? Because she isn't the one getting married. Ticking all those 'must do' boxes. There's no easy way. Thandi's foot is tapping on the living room floor. She changes her sitting position to cross legged. Evie's back in the rattan chair now. She looks at Evie in her off the shoulder baby pink maxi dress.

'Hang on, is that what you were wearing? This morning?'

'Yes, nothing in particular,' Evie says.

'Evie, I've got it now. That fashion brand of nothing in particular makes complete strangers come up to you in record stores and fall at your feet. That's it. Simple as.'

She checks herself. She's fallen into that trap of questioning what a woman wears. It's going to be a long afternoon. Evie's completely off topic. And the encounter with this man in Mabu's doesn't make sense. Doesn't make sense *yet*. She'll have to wait. This will be the prequel. There no shortcuts with Evie when it comes to getting to the point of a story. It'll be in there somewhere. Just need to wait, she tells herself. Thandi makes the time out signal and heads to the kitchen.

From the living room, Evie hears Thandi slowing lunch down. For a few seconds, she listens, trying to work out if the noise level is normal Thandi or annoyed Thandi. It's somewhere in between. For months, Thandi's been saying she's fine, but Evie knows she isn't. There's something wrong and it's not just because Evie's late. She's always late. Everyone knows that. She can hear Thandi on the phone now, talking to Nadine. Saying something about the Evie Show. Ouch, she says to herself. Well, the Evie Show has always been another running joke in their friendship group. Thandi usually says she's only teasing when she says that. But it doesn't feel like that this afternoon. Sometimes Thandi has impossible standards to live up to. And she's been so serious lately. Evie knows there's work to be done for next week. But we don't have to be serious all the time, do we?

'By the way, it wasn't entirely my fault that I ended up in Mabu's,' she says, calling out to Thandi in the kitchen.

If I start again, it might help, Evie says to herself. She needs to get to the real point of the story. She's not quite ready to say it out loud. But it's been on her mind for a couple of months now. Then Thandi broke up with Julius. Didn't think it was the right time to talk about her problems. Which is why she's waited. Why she's here today. As well as to help Thandi with the protest march preparations, she reminds herself.

Evie thinks back to the morning at Mabu's when she'd passed quickly through Soul, Funk, Latin, New Age, Electronic, Disco and Fusion. She ticks them off in her head. It was when she got to Jazz that she was side-tracked. She'd suddenly thought of another Miles Davis record that she'd been meaning to buy. The record store was busy. People passing through. Deliveries. Boxes being unloaded. She watches as Thandi comes back into the living room holding a bottle of white wine.

'So I heard a thud,' Evie says, continuing her story. 'I looked around. There was a man getting to his feet.

Someone was helping him up. Before I knew it, he was standing right by me, patting himself down, checking his hands for cuts. Said it must have been a box sticking out that he hadn't seen.'

Evie remembers he stood tall, rolling his shoulders and neck. She'd noticed his Veja shoes, his woven bracelets on his wrists as he flicked through the vinyls beside her.

'Thandi, it wasn't anything I was wearing,' Evie says. 'It was obvious he was looking for something specific. Of course, it had crossed my mind he might not know anything about jazz. I'm not that stupid.'

The comment about her clothing has irritated her. What does Thandi always say I am? Gullible. I'm not *that* gullible.

'Anyway, he finally said something to me. He pulled out a record. Said it should be in the bottom half of the alphabet where I was,' Evie says. 'You'll never guess what record it was.'

Thandi shakes her head.

'It was *Grazing in the Grass: The Best of Hugh Masekela*. You know. Hugh Masekela. He died not so long ago. So, I took it from him and slipped it into M. Then he asked if I was into jazz. He said something about the intro on the opening track. The bell and the drums. He did some air drumming. Like this.'

Evie imitates the intro for Thandi.

'I could tell he knew the music perfectly. And then he said something else.' Evie turns to look out of the window. 'Let me think. That's it. You don't always need words when you listen to something like that.'

She can tell from Thandi's face that hasn't gone down well. She wasn't expecting their conversation to be so scratchy. They've never been scratchy. Evie remembers there's something else she needs from her bag. She walks across the living room. Should have shown this to Thandi as soon as she arrived. She takes out her iPad, flips open the cover, quickly taps the screen and hands it to Thandi on the sofa. They sit side by side.

'Anyway, I thought you might like some help with the designs for the t-shirts. For next week,' Evie says. 'Couldn't sleep last night.'

It's not like Evie to have a bad night's sleep, Thandi thinks, taking the iPad. Evie can sleep standing up. As she swipes through the t-shirt designs, she feels a ridiculous sense of relief. These past few months, Thandi's realised she's been keeping a scorecard of their friendship. It's a sure sign of being out of touch. Out of synch. Of worrying about being let down, of not being important anymore. Thandi puts the iPad on the sofa, goes to the mantelpiece and grabs two wine glasses. She unscrews the top of the wine bottle.

'They're brilliant Evie,' Thandi says. 'I really like the font you've chosen. The colours. And the way you've set the silhouettes of the girls' faces with their names. Our message couldn't be clearer.'

Our message. She likes the sound of that. Thandi pours the wine. 'The next thing we need to do is go through all the names to be printed on the backs of the t-shirts.'

She hands Evie a glass. That's so Evie, she says to

herself. Always pulls a rabbit out of the hat when you least expect it. Anyway, she's delayed Nadine. It'll give her a bit more time just to be with Evie and catch up with her once she's got through this crazy story.

'So...' Thandi says, sinking slowly back into the cushions on the sofa. 'Tell me...'

'So... Jacques, that's his name. We just started talking about music. You know what it's like? Well, I asked him what he was listening to. He had his air pods with him. Said he was listening to Solange. You know the song, I'm sure you do. It's been around for a while. I'll play it for you now,' Evie says.

She takes out her phone and scrolls quickly through her playlists.

'It's one of the best break-up songs ever. Losing You. Filmed the music video here in C.T. Well, not exactly here. But out in the Cape Flats. In Langa, in fact.'

'Maybe, that's a sign he's broken up with someone,' Thandi says, standing and walking to her desk in the corner of the living room. 'Not good if he's on the rebound, heh?'

Funny. She and Julius never really talked about music. They listened to their own and then found something in the middle, some easy listening, for when they cooked together or were in the car driving somewhere. Anyway, she shakes her head, she doesn't want to think of Julius and their breakup. Or his message that he'd sent earlier today. He got too serious. Too quickly. Just didn't want that. And no, it wasn't okay to have his three-year-old along on dates. She was not going to be a step-mommy yet. All that pressure she feels about being in her thirties. The biological clock ticking. What did Nadine say? We're born with a million eggs, Thandi, and we won't get any more. We're losing them by the hour. How could anyone think that was a good idea?

Thandi glances at Evie, imagining her in a few years' time with a baby, frazzled, nothing left to talk about, muslin cloths draped over her shoulder, protecting her clothes. How can she tell Evie that all those trappings of marriage and love are not for her? At least, not for a while. And thinking about Julius doesn't help. That's another difference between her and Evie. When she's in a relationship she always expects it to go wrong; whereas Evie always thinks it will work out and they will live happily ever after. Being single is good, she reminds herself. It's good. I am a complete adult. Rinse repeat. I am a complete adult.

From her desk in the corner of the living room, Thandi picks up a brown manila folder, filled with newspaper cuttings and printed out online news reports. She reads through the list of names of the women they have so far.

'Anyway, talking about the Cape Flats. You know that's where they found the last woman?' Thandi says, turning to Evie.

It was the final straw for Thandi. It made her start to organise the protest. She'd had enough. Personal security was a constant topic of concern and conversation in their friendship group. It was becoming frightening. Out of control. Still is. No one doing anything about it. She wasn't expecting to get so caught up with it. To be the driving force. Taking things into her own hands. Not being able to think about anything else once she got going. She brings the file back to the sofa.

Thandi's right, Evie says to herself, as she looks at her flicking through the file on the sofa. What on earth am I going on about? She thinks of Langa, one of the oldest townships in Cape Town. A fifteen-minute drive away. She's been there. To some of the shebeens to listen to music. Evie takes a sip of wine. Anyway, it's not Jacques she really needs to talk about. It's the row with René, that's where she needs to start. Rows. Plural. At the beginning. It's hard to put it all into words. And say it out loud that maybe René's… Evie yawns.

She didn't get to sleep until past one o'clock. Slept on the sofa. The row last night was on her mind when she was in Mabu's this morning. She was tired. Quietly flicking through vinyls, the soft sound as she went from one to the next and the micro puff of air that rose as one leaned into the other, was just what she needed before heading up to Thandi's for a heart to heart. Evie's noticed, since the breakup with Julius, Thandi doesn't ask her about the wedding. If she did, she might have started to say something earlier.

'I did actually walk off, you know when Jacques started talking to me, I picked up my bag and went to the Folk section. To find the Joni record,' Evie says. 'It got broken.'

She notices Thandi sitting up now, on the sofa.

'I can't live without that record, knowing it's in pieces. Unplayable. I had to replace it,' Evie says.

'So, what happened?'

'He followed me to Folk.'

Thandi curls back up on the sofa, tucking her legs under her. She waits. She takes a sip of wine. She's thinking about what Evie has just said. When she asked Evie what had happened, she meant what had happened to the Joni record.

'Evie, don't you think that's a bit creepy he followed you there?' Thandi says.

Evie doesn't answer.

'So you're now in Folk. He's followed you. Because he has a sudden interest in what? Joni Mitchell?' Thandi says. 'No man ever admits to listening to Joni Mitchell.'

Thandi thinks of René. She's decided. She's not going to say anything. It's not her relationship. It's Evie's life. She's just going to be happy for Evie. What's so wrong about boring steady love? Except, as she looks at Evie, she doesn't seem that happy.

'Okay, my beautiful friend,' Thandi says. 'Don't tell me this Jacques guy wears Veja shoes *and* listens to Joni Mitchell? You'll be telling me next he's a feminist and you've recruited him for the march next week?'

They laugh. Now, that would be good. The laughter has helped. It might make their conversation like old times, when they shared an apartment together, when they were both single. When they shared everything except their moon cups. They drew a line at that.

As Thandi fills up their wine glasses again, she thinks about Julius's message. She's left it on read.

'Jacques asked me what music I was looking for. But I didn't really want to answer at first. Once you start talking about music, it reveals everything about you, doesn't it?' Evie says.

Thandi isn't so sure. She's always been a made especially for you by an algorithm kind of girl. Loves it when a new playlist lands in her inbox.

'And then what?' Thandi says.

'I went and had a coffee with him.'

Thandi rolls her eyes and sighs. 'Why do you always think that life is all neat, candy-coated and tied up with a bow. Like…' she says and waves her hand as she thinks, '…you know. Like an Ed Sheeran song.' She pauses.

'And, Evie,' Thandi adds, weighing her words carefully, realising she's about to change her mind again. 'What I do know is that you're supposed to be marrying René. Remember? The man of your dreams. And you don't know a thing about this man, Jacques, you met only four hours ago. What's going on?'

She watches Evie. She can tell she's uncomfortable by the way she's playing with her hair. Thandi gets up and goes back to the kitchen feeling annoyed. A chat in a record store is one thing, in a crowded place. But to then go off for a coffee with a stranger when she's also meant to be meeting me? She finds what she's looking for and comes back to the living room with a newspaper.

'Did you hear about this one ?' Thandi says, holding up the newspaper. 'We're all targets. It could be you. It could be me next time. If we're not careful.'

Thandi hears a shrill tone creeping into her voice. She thinks about next week's protest march. What's the point of wearing a t-shirt with a slogan and a hashtag on it? It's not going to solve anything.

'Your Mabu dreamboat is probably out there now, followed you up the hill to my house. He's outside, in Bo-Kaap, waiting for you. Have you thought of that? That he targeted you in Mabu's?'

She points out the living room window.

'Well, at least check him out online. Suppose you've looked at his socials?' Thandi says.

Evie shakes her head. She doesn't know Jacques's socials. She'd meant to ask him when they'd had coffee together. They'd only exchanged mobile numbers. There wasn't time for a quick check and balance of personal facts—where he lives, where he works. She knew she was already running seriously late for lunch.

'I had a sixth sense about Jacques,' Evie says, then regrets it. It's exactly what she shouldn't say to Thandi, the bullshit detector.

'Evie, there's no such thing. Instant attraction is a chemical reaction like taking cocaine. It has the same effect in the brain,' Thandi says, straight back.

It had all happened so fast. Too fast, Evie knows that. Thandi's right. What was she thinking? Her phone vibrates. There's a message. It's from Jacques. No, she was right. She did have a sixth sense. She opens the message. It's a playlist. She clicks on the link. Yes. It's got all the music they'd chatted about. They'd also talked about the dance tempo of Solange's Losing You. She quickly scans the rest of the music. There's more, he's added. She reads *Jacques… typing*. He's sending her another message. She opens it. There's a photo of her

199

mohair cardigan.

'Oh,' Evie says.

She shows Thandi the photo on her phone.

'Thought I'd lost it,' she says. 'Must have left it on the chair beside me when we'd gone for a coffee.'

She avoids looking at Thandi.

'We only went to the café, just next door to Mabu's. It was busy. I didn't want to go far,' Evie says. 'Didn't want to be late.'

How do I explain it all to Thandi? That's the problem. She thinks back to what Jacques said about jazz. How you don't need words, you just need to listen to the music. It tells you everything. But she must put it into words. Words for René for starters. She thinks back over the past couple of months when the doubts started to creep in about getting married. Couldn't commit to a date let alone canapés. She sees Thandi raise her left hand and point at her engagement finger.

'You know, at first, I couldn't get my ring off. Stuck! I had to hold my arm above my head. I did that as I walked up the hill to here.'

She shows Thandi what she did, raising her arm. She takes the ring out of her dress pocket and puts it on top of *Song to a Seagull*, on the coffee table.

'Evie! Since when? Not since this morning? Surely not. You can't do that over a man you've only just met.'

'There's something I need to tell you. I should have said this at the beginning. But you know what I'm like. So, I'm going to double back now.' Evie pauses. 'René deliberately broke the record. He said he didn't. But he did. It doesn't matter now because actually I've been having doubts for months. And kept ignoring them. Then he said his job was moving to Jo'burg. And all the questions I keep getting asked about the wedding are piling up. And piling up.'

Evie picks up her wine glass.

'You were right, Thandi. I've just got to get bigger dreams.'

They sit in silence for a moment, words hanging in the air like the scent of the white lilies.

Bigger dreams? Thandi feels a bloom of heat go through her. Yes, those were her exact words. No need to worry about being honest with Evie this afternoon. She'd already done that a while back. Evie's phone rings. Thandi watches her answer it. She knows who it is from the ringtone.

'Yes, yes. I'm fine,' Evie says, into her mobile. 'I can't really talk right now. Yes. Let's meet. Okay. We do need to talk... I guess you're right. Later... I'm not sure when... In a couple of hours? At the Waterfront? Yes. See you then.'

Evie puts her phone down on her lap. Thandi has a feeling Evie's close to the beginning of the story.

'Do you remember what Joni Mitchell said when she went up the aisle?'

Thandi shakes her head.

'So, legend has it, that when Joni went up the aisle to get married, she said to herself, you can always get out of this.' Evie takes a sip of wine. 'Well, that's what I always thought when I got engaged to René. That's how I think about most things in life.'

For a few moments, she sits back and thinks of the

headlines in the newspaper that Thandi has just shown her. She looks at the 'sorry for being late' flowers in the vase. She looks across at Thandi. No, on second thoughts, she's going to stay. There's work to be done. Important work.

'Give me a minute, Thandi.'

She messages René to tell him she's got a lot on this afternoon. She can't make it tonight. She'll meet him tomorrow. Just needs a little more time. With Thandi. Except she doesn't say that bit in the message. Evie scrolls through her phone, searching for the Joni song that will explain everything. She finds it. Presses play. Thandi waits. She hears the familiar sound of the acoustic guitar come soaring through the speakers. Evie points to the air above her head to get Thandi's attention. It's the end of the first verse of Cactus Tree, the line that's repeated throughout the song, that Evie waits for, that she wants Thandi to hear. Ah, here it comes.

'Just listen,' she says.

Thandi sits back, picking out each word, each line of the song that she knows so well but hasn't heard for a while. She looks at Evie across the room, catching her eye. She knows what Evie's thinking. What she's been trying to say. It's like the old days, when a quick glance at a dinner table, a raised eyebrow across a dance floor, those silent codes of friendship, say everything.

'Turn it up!' Thandi says.

She hears three words at the end of the first verse. Busy being free. Should she mention to Evie that she's thinking of moving to Paris?

202

Heavenly phoenix on earth

There's a thin line of pain running from Philip's scapula up through his neck to the back of his skull. It's been an uncomfortable night. He's barely slept. For a split second, he's confused where he is. He can feel the wooden arm rests, the soft spongey upholstered seat beneath him, a cushion in the small of his back. The layer of smells confirms it. I made it, he says to himself as he opens his eyes and recognises his mother's bedroom in the nursing home.

The journey last night flashes through Philip's head. He knew he was cutting it fine. The run across the station concourse. The small boy he sent flying. A man, probably the father, shouting and pointing an imaginary gun at him. Yes, the man fired at him. To cap it all, the blue balloon that floated slowly up to the roof of Paddington station. Don't say it was the boy's birthday. Philip groans. Yes, he was a first-class shit in a suit. But he had to get the train. The last train of the day. Perhaps the very last one he would ever have to catch to

Taunton.

It's early. He hears his mother's shallow breathing and the ticking of the clock. The soft sunlight of early summer creeps slowly along the floor, the walls, his mother's bed, across her long still body and the sleeves of her blue nightdress, catching the gold of her wedding ring. As the light intensifies, so does the bird song. What a glorious distraction from the present, he thinks. He watches his mother, her chest moving evenly with each intake of breath.

'Are you awake?' Philip says. 'I'm here. I'm back.'

Hearing is the last sense that goes. Vilma, the nursing home manager, told him that in the call yesterday when she said to come straightaway. His mother had suddenly deteriorated. He needed to come. Code for she didn't think it would be long. Philip had dropped everything. She'd said to him, if your mother's calm and not agitated, keep talking. Read her something. The sound of your voice is reassuring. She'll know it's you.

It was only a month ago they were Netflix junkies, hooked on the Chinese drama *Ten Miles of Peach Blossoms*. Now, Philip's facing perhaps a final conversation.

It's funny how time doesn't fly when someone's dying, Philip thinks as he looks at the clock. Time's yawningly slow, the past mingling with the present, the future a growing shadow. With all the dashes up and down to Taunton, he's spent a lot of time staring out of windows and thinking about his childhood. It's like a magic carpet. It keeps following him. It takes him off to places he's forgotten or hasn't thought about for years. His early childhood is exactly what Philip wants to talk about with his mother. Being an only child, there's no one else. His memories are blurry, imprecise, layered. He puts his hand gently on his mother, feeling the rise and fall of her breath. It reminds him of when his children were babies, always checking their breathing. He drags his chair to the bed to be as close as possible. He knows where he wants to start.

'Do you remember the Chow Chows when we lived in Hong Kong? Do you remember them? I thought they were lions at first. Pet lions. I was obsessed with them. They used to tiptoe along as if their tiny feet had been bound in cloth.'

Philip has a vivid image in his mind of the dogs' comical way of walking.

'I used to love going up high into the mountain behind our flat. I used to think a beautiful princess lived up there with her lion dogs.'

Philip knows he must keep talking.

'Once, I took you to the window at the back of the flat, to show you the house with the Chow Chows. I used to call it the Forbidden Palace. What was I then? About eight or nine? The dogs were always far too regal to ever put their paws on the grass. Not even to shit. I said they were orange. And then I changed my mind and said they were the colour of amber, like amber in the typhoon signals. Pinkie and I loved those dogs.'

He stops his story. Ah Pinkie, he hasn't thought about Pinkie for a long time. He can see her now. Pudding bowl haircut. Total dare-devil. Complete opposite to him. He can see that now.

'But the Chow Chows, that's the English name. It's the Chinese name for them I've been trying to remember.'

For months, Philip's been mulling over memories of his early childhood. He's been trying to loosen the tight knot in his head, to unravel the strands and lay them out neatly and clearly. But he knows it can't be done. At least, not on his own. Life isn't like pieces of Lego that can be independently examined and scrutinised and then slotted all perfectly together. For a few moments, Philip taps the side of his head with his finger, trying to dig out the words for the dogs in Chinese. It's no good.

'Do you remember what Chow Chows are called? Their name in Chinese?'

He wants his mother to respond, to react, to engage in any small way with him. The words for the dogs elude him but they're there, somewhere in his memory bank. He can feel them. They're coming now. Almost on the tip of his tongue. They'll come. Or his mother will know. She'll know. He's sure of that.

A wave of exhaustion wafts over him. It has the heaviness of jet lag. He tries to fight it. The room's hot and stuffy. He's tired from his late-night dash and broken sleep. Through the bedroom door, he hears someone setting out thick china cups and saucers on a trolley. He stands, takes a sip of water and opens the window wide. He drums his feet, rubs his eyes and sits back down in the chair, telling himself he mustn't fall asleep, especially not now. Time's not on his side. But his eyelids close like shutters. Philip surrenders, drifting off into a deep sleep, picturing the Chow Chows, panting in the heat of Hong Kong, blue tongues hanging down like aged raw steak.

'Fahrenheit. Fahrenheit. Do you read me? Over.'

Crouched on the exposed rock, Philip's eyes sweep the terrain. He's holding a small black walkie-talkie to his ear, his notebook at his feet. Being up on the mountain makes him feel like an emperor as he surveys his realm, from the top of Hong Kong Island down to the South China Sea.

'Fahrenheit. Fahrenheit. Do you read me? Over.'

'I can hear you,' a voice says. 'The whole world can hear you. You're echoing down the mountain.'

Philip spins round.

'Where were you? I was trying to get you. The typhoon's coming. We need to hurry.'

Fahrenheit shrugs and waggles a walkie-talkie in front of his face.

'Batteries. They're bust,' she says. 'Corroded. Humidity got to them. I found this on the way up here. Taaa daaaa!' She holds up a long translucent snakeskin. 'Cobra! You can tell. It's nearly as tall as me. Do you want to keep it?'

Philip shakes his head.

'I brought these along too.' Fahrenheit unbuckles the top of a satchel and pulls out a small pair of binoculars. He snatches them.

'Careful! They're not mine. I'll get roasted if something happens to them,' Fahrenheit says.

Philip puts the binoculars to his eyes, training his

sightline on the Forbidden Palace with its tall perimeter fence. He finds the dogs, Ming and Tang. He inspects each Chow Chow from top to toe. He starts with their small triangular-shaped ears, set above a heavy square face, with their black currant eyes. He moves along their stocky golden frame to their upright tails curling above their haunches. Just like lions.

The children squat in silence, boiling with the heat of the rock radiating through the soles of their sandals. They hug their knees to their chests and wipe sweat from the crease in their forearms. It's a waiting game.

'Aaaaah. The bloodsuckers got me,' Fahrenheit says, flapping a hand angrily, legs flaying, feet stamping on the dark red ants until they look like crushed berries.

'Shhh. The dogs will hear us. Look. Ming's lifted her head already.'

'But we're too far away.'

'No, we're not. They're guard dogs. They're protecting their mistress. They can hear everything we do. They can smell us.'

Fahrenheit squats back down on the rock and opens the satchel again. 'Cigarette?'

Philip looks at Fahrenheit holding the red and white packet.

'Don't worry. My dad has lots. Boxes and boxes of them.'

They light their cigarettes, catching each other's eyes. They give the signal of a double raised eyebrow and sing the TV advertising jingle 'Winston tastes good, like a cigarette should!' They snigger. But they keep their eyes pinned on the Forbidden Palace and the Chow Chows.

They watch Ming who sits up slowly and eases herself to her feet. The dog strolls across the veranda, sits again and slides along the white tiles, using the pads on her front paws to steady her speed. She lands smoothly in a full stretch. Tang lies on his side panting. Philip makes notes.

'I love them,' says Fahrenheit.

'Same.'

The children hear a low sound. They nudge each other. They know where it's coming from. It's the glass door. It's moving. Somebody's sliding it.

'See. I told you last time when we saw the face at the window. I said she'd come outside,' Fahrenheit says. 'I don't think she ever leaves. In fact, she's probably a prisoner, kept against her will by her evil father, the emperor. Her stepmother keeps her chained to the wall until she dies of starvation and then the maggots will eat her. Even her eyeballs.' Fahrenheit pauses. 'I think she's a whore.'

Philip stubs his cigarette on the rock.

'Maybe.'

A woman's head peers out. The Chow Chows sit up.

Was that a knock at the bedroom door? Philip opens his eyes. He isn't sure. Something or someone's woken him. It takes a few seconds to orientate himself back to the present. He's right. Someone's been in the room. Probably one of the carers. Things have moved. It'll be a humanoid robot by the time I'm in a nursing home, he thinks. He looks across at his mother. The bed clothes have been tidied and straightened. There's a cup of tea at his side. He reaches for it. Cold. He pours himself another glass of water, takes a sip and clears his throat. He looks at the clock. He pictures the Forbidden Palace, the white house up the mountain and the sliding door.

Across the room, Philip sees the small rosewood Chinese chest with its warm burgundy hue and wash of dark veining. It belongs to his mother. It's like an old childhood friend. His eyes trace its sweeping intricate mother of pearl in-lay of a peacock that begins on the lid and goes down the front like a waterfall. Philip loved the peacock carving as a boy. He stands and walks quietly across the room. His eyes follow the outline of the peacock sitting in a tree, with one hundred eyes in its long magical tail. He takes the slim rectangular brass lock in his hand. But Philip hesitates. It wasn't that he wasn't allowed to look in the chest. He just never did.

Philip pops the lock open and slides it off. He lifts the heavy small lid. The scalloped brass latch tinkles as it flops forwards. Philip rests the lid against the wall. And there it is. He breathes in deeply. He inhales the potent, fragrant, antiseptic smell. Camphor! The smell catches the back of his throat and the inside of his nostrils.

'Can you smell it?' He says to his mother, rubbing his nose. 'The camphor?'

Philip loved the smell as a child. Camphor now reminds him of hospitals. He looks again at the mother of pearl peacock on the rosewood chest. He knows the peacock is a symbol for dignity and beauty, the heavenly phoenix on earth. He's trying to recall its name in

Chinese, like the Chow Chows. He knew the words once. His mother would know. She was the linguist in the family.

At the top of the chest, Philip sees a small hardback book. He recognises the front cover, with its illustrations of pearl fishermen, of monster catfish with long whiskers, of princesses in silky gowns with long floaty ribbons and emperors with forbidding beards dressed in gold brocade. He picks the book up and opens it. The spine's loose. Pages fall open like a cookery book to a much-loved recipe. He closes it and sniffs the top of the spine. Camphor again!

Sitting down with the book, Philip suddenly has an idea. He turns the pages, reading the familiar titles of the folk tales The Missing Axe, Li Chi Slays the Serpent, The Silkworm Goddess. He nods away to himself as he searches for his favourite story. It's in there somewhere. When he finds it, he taps the opening paragraph.

'I'll read this to you,' he says to his mother. 'Wu Gang and the Magic Tree'.

He scans the words, the number of pages, and reads: 'Long ago, there was a village in China by the banks of the Yellow River. It was a very poor village. Everyone who lived there was always on the verge of starvation. Floods from the river would devastate the crops.'

He turns to his mother. He watches the rise and fall of her breathing. She must be listening, he thinks. He continues reading how hard Wu Gang and his poor family worked sowing rice crops in the paddy fields. He gets to the part when the sparrow brought Wu Gang the magic seed.

'Do you remember what happens next in the story?'

Philip feels his mother squeeze his hand. The lightest of pressure. His mother is conscious. She's listening to all his nervous chatter about the Chow Chows, Pinkie and the Forbidden Palace. She's listening to the story of Wu Gang, the lazy woodcutter. She squeezes his hand once more, her fingers pressing into Philip's palm. Vilma's right. You're still with me. Somehow, holding her hand makes him feel that he's tethering her to the present.

'Here's a question for you. Do you remember what peacock is in Chinese? You were always the one who was good at Chinese,' Philip says, glancing back to the chest across the room.

He feels another gentle squeeze.

'You do? Give me a second... I think I do too. The word for peacock. The heavenly phoenix on earth... Yes! Kǒng què.'

His mother squeezes his hand.

'Kǒng què,' Philip says again.

He smiles. Two words that connect him and his mother. In this moment. To another moment. Funny that. He picks the book up again and carries on reading the story, how Wu Gang was banished to the moon. He knows it by heart. He doesn't even really need the book. It makes him think of Pinkie again and how they used to act out the story and often changed bits. Sometimes Pinkie was Wu Gang, and sometimes Philip was. It was their game, their secret, their world.

'You know, I always thought I could see Wu Gang

when I looked up at the moon,' Philip says, turning to his mother and closing the book. 'And the Jade Rabbit.'

He listens again to her breathing and the clock ticking beside her bed. It's feeling almost normal, sitting in this room, reading a childhood story. He hears his mother's voice. A tiny murmur. He stands up quickly to get closer to her. The book falls to the floor.

'What did you say?'

He leans over and bends his head to hers.

'Tell me again. I'm listening.'

Philip waits. No, he's missed it. She's silent again. He sits back down. He looks out of the bedroom window. Watches the birds racing across the lawn: blackbirds, speckled thrushes and blue tits. A squirrel climbs the bird table, ready to raid the tubes of sunflower seeds. He watches it hang upside down and work its way in. So English, he thinks. He sits back in the chair.

The sliding door is now open. Fahrenheit stands, looking through the binoculars. Philip takes out his surveillance notebook and pen to make an entry on today's sightings.

'Stay down low,' he tells Fahrenheit. 'If you get spotted, we'll be in big trouble. Now, tell me what you see. I need to record it all properly. I've already got Ming and Tang down in my notebook.'

This is the fifth sighting of the Chow Chows. He knows five is a lucky number. He puts a large asterisk by the date.

'Hurry up!' Philip says, looking up to the sky.

It's thick and grey. The typhoon's coming. The wind's

getting stronger. They need to hurry and get back down the mountain before the rain comes. Fahrenheit is silent. Philip waits, tapping his pen on his notebook. They've been waiting all summer for this moment to solve the mystery of the woman at the window. With the door opening and a glimpse of the woman's face, he knows they could be close to the answer.

Philip hears Fahrenheit's low whistle. It's the signal for when something really important happens.

'Jackpot. Jackpot,' Fahrenheit whispers.

'Shut up. We'll get spotted. The dogs will hear us.'

'But we've hit the jackpot,' Fahrenheit says again. 'You've got to see this.'

Philip stops writing.

'The woman. I need to tell you about the woman,' Fahrenheit says. 'The woman's Chinese. I'm sure she's the face we've always seen at the window. She's got really long hair. She's wearing… something with long sleeves.' Fahrenheit looks through the binoculars again. 'I think it's a kimono. It's blue. But she's not out yet. She's still at the window. Hang on a sec. She's calling Ming and Tang over.'

The dogs start to bark.

'That's us they're barking at. They've smelt us. They've heard you,' Philip says, looking up at the sky. 'Fahrenheit, it's going to rain. The typhoon's coming.'

'Phil… Phil…' Fahrenheit says.

'Don't call me that.'

'But Phil!'

'Okay. That's it, Fahrenheit. That's three rules you've broken today. No walkie-talkie. No camouflage. And you're not even using my secret agent name. You've ruined it. I'm going down now. Make your own way back. I don't know why I let you into this game.'

Philip stands and snaps his notebook closed. He puts it in his pocket with his pen. He looks at the darkening clouds. The typhoon is fast approaching. He can see it over the South China Sea. He grabs the cobra skin and walks off quickly without looking back.

'But the woman,' Fahrenheit calls out after him. 'Don't you want to know about the woman? She's just come out. Out onto the veranda. I can see her.'

Philip doesn't reply. He's walking down the path.

'She's in a wheelchair. She's a…'

Fifty years later, the word echoes in Philip's head as he looks out into the garden. Pinkie's voice is crystal clear. The word is crystal clear. He remembers hearing it as he stomped off, how it bounced down the mountain after him, like a stone ricocheting off the mountain side, chasing him. Philip shifts in his armchair. He mouths the word: spastic. Did the woman hear it? Now he knows he isn't dreaming or making up this bit of his childhood. He can tell by the tight pit in his stomach. He hasn't thought about this in decades. Philip stands and gives himself a shake, trying to rid himself of the uncomfortable memory, the lingering shame. He walks back across the room to his mother's rosewood chest.

Kneeling, he opens it. The latch tinkles. The smell of camphor returns. He feels around in the chest and lifts out a pair of sandals. He holds up the gold zoris and rubs his fingers along the small dainty red and green jewels attached to the straps. Funny to keep these. He has a flashback. A pair of men's shoes, black lace-ups. He shakes his head. Where's that come from? All this time travelling has been unsettling. He works his way down to the bottom of the chest. His hand touches on something. He pulls it out. It's a brocade jewellery case. He unties the ribbon and unfolds it.

'My surveillance notebook,' he says, picking it up.

He opens it. Pages slip out.

'So that's where it went. It vanished into thin air. Couldn't find it anywhere. I always thought you kept it. Or Mei had thrown it away. But Mei wouldn't have done that, would she?' He says to his mother.

Philip walks into the kitchen and holds up the cobra skin. Mei stands there with her arms crossed over her white cheongsam and black trousers, her long hair the colour of ash scraped back and tied in a bun at the back of her head, hairpin speared through.

'Bad boy. Typhoon coming,' Mei says. 'And snakes! They come. Eat you. Then you dead.'

She opens her mouth wide and raises her arms, like a monster. Philip can see her gold tooth at the back of her mouth.

'A cobra doesn't do that, Mei. And that's a python that swallows its prey in one go.'

Mei's face looks fierce.

'Lunch not ready. You early.' Mei sniffs the air, pointing to the invisible smells coming off the cooker and from the oven.

Philip sniffs too. He's hungry. He walks through the

swing door, hearing it swish along the floor. The large formal table in the dining room is laid for one, with his favourite rice bowl with the golden dragon motif, chopsticks and rice spoon.

'Boy! Boy!' Mei calls.

What does Mei want now? He still needs to check for intruders. He does that every time he's been up the mountain. Philip spots the ashtray on the sitting room windowsill. He sees two cigarette stubs lying in the heavy clear glass, one with a ring of fuchsia pink lipstick around the filter. There's an opened packet of cigarettes on the rosewood chest. He takes out his notebook, flips back a few pages and records the date, the time and what he sees. He goes to the front door to check if his mother's zoris are there. He hears Mei shouting again. He stands looking at the shoes. His mother's zoris. Heavy black lace-ups. The usuals. He writes a few more details in his notebook. He hears a familiar but crackly voice.

'Fahrenheit to Base. Fahrenheit to Base. Over.'

Mei's standing in the sitting room holding his walkie-talkie. She's rolling her eyes.

'Your spy friend,' she says.

Philip runs and snatches the walkie-talkie from Mei. He switches it off and throws it on a chair. He's still furious with Pinkie. He wants to find his mother. He wants to talk to her. He walks down the corridor. The bedroom door is closed.

'Mummy resting,' Mei says.

She's standing at the other end of the corridor. She puts a finger to her lips, then beckons him to the kitchen. He walks back down the corridor and follows Mei through the sitting room. He notices the ashtray has gone. And the cigarettes. He looks at the front door. The black shoes have gone too. He walks into the kitchen, takes out his notebook and adds the information.

'Boy. You be careful,' Mei says. 'Many spies in China. Red Guard come and take you.' She drags a finger across her throat and shows him the whites of her eyes. 'Now, sit!' she says, bringing out a tall white plastic stool.

She picks up a parcel wrapped in newspaper and lets it fall with a thud on the kitchen counter in front of him. She unwraps it. A dead chicken rolls out.

'Nice. Fresh. Killed this morning at the market. You help Mei-Mei.'

Mei opens a drawer. She takes out a wooden board and a polished stainless-steel chopper with a rectangular blade the size of her hand. She picks up the carcass and drops it on the board. Holding the chopper up high, she brings it down with a single stroke across the chicken's neck.

'There. Chairman Mao. Dead.' She points at the headless chicken and laughs. 'Boy, your turn. Take feet off. We cook them later.'

Philip wriggles off his stool and comes around to Mei's side. He picks up the chopper, feeling the heavy head of the blade in his hand. Weight forwards. Quick clean action. He thinks of the black shoes as he brings the chopper down. He cuts off the feet. Intruder. Dead. A blue bottle hovers over the carcass. Mei wafts it away with her hand. The milky green of her jade bracelet is flecked with specks of dark crimson blood. He reaches across to her wrist and wipes the blood away with his finger. He feels the smooth stone as he circles the bracelet clean, so cool in the humidity of the kitchen. Mei rubs his head and pulls him towards her. He feels the crisp starchiness of her uniform and the soft belly against his cheek.

'Why you like Pinkie so much? Why you keep playing with her?' Mei says. 'She much too clever for you.'

As Philip gazes through the bedroom window, he knows Mei was right about Pinkie. Far too clever for him. He never spoke to Pinkie again after the row. He thinks about his mother's closed bedroom door, the ash tray, the notebook that disappeared, and the black shoes he can't explain. Why did Pinkie try and call him on the walkie-talkie after they'd had that row up the mountain? The magic carpet of childhood now feels like a moped gang that's pursuing him.

Philip picks up his old surveillance notebook and opens it. The memory of the young Chinese woman shames him. He was only interested in the Chow Chows at the Forbidden Palace. It was Pinkie who was hell-bent on finding out about the woman. It was her idea. It was her stupid game. She was always the first to say, let's go up the mountain to the Forbidden Palace.

His mother stirs a little.

'It's funny. I've just found my old notebook. You remember the notebook, don't you?'

Philip looks out of the window. He's thinking. You took it from me, one school holiday, he says to himself. I couldn't work out why. But I remember I was furious. He flips to the beginning of the notebook, to the first pages, looking at the other entries he made about the intruder. Like the sightings of the Chow Chows, the dates and times are precisely recorded. Philip can see the pattern in the entries. He closes the notebook and taps it on his open palm. He goes over the details in his mind again. It's there in black and white. It must be true, mustn't it? The details of the intruders match his trips up the mountain to spy on the Forbidden Palace. All of a sudden, his mother's interest in where he went as a small boy in the school holidays doesn't feel like maternal concern.

But who had all the cigarettes? Boxes and boxes of Winston cigarettes? Philip glances at his mother as he thinks back to his childhood. He pictures Pinkie and him puffing away on the stolen stash on the rock. He shakes his head. Surely not. It can't be. He doesn't want to think about it. Now is not the time. He can't have been the only one who was lonely. His father was away a lot. He hears his mother trying to say something. Philip leans over the bed to listen to her.

'I'm here,' Philips says to her.

He takes his mother's hand. His mother says something again. It's a whisper. Philip's close enough to hear her. Now he knows she's heard every word he's spoken this morning. She's been following Philip from the moment he started talking about the Chow Chows. He feels her squeezing his hand. She repeats the words.

He's got them. He leans back in his chair.

'Sōng shī quǎn,' Philip says.

He looks out the window at the garden, at the sun that's now rising high into the sky, the birds belting across the view.

'That's what the Chow Chows are called in Chinese. Such beautiful words for such beautiful creatures,' he says.

Sōng shī quǎn.

Acknowledgements

My thanks to all those who read early drafts of stories and answered my questions. Any errors that still exist are mine: Ira Jankowski, Joanne Ashcroft, Subhasree Biswas, Geoffrey Charin, Sam Martin Burr, Philip Farrugia Randon, David Marriott, Joas Kamps, Mustafa Marwan, Soledad Riestra and Stuart Lee.

Mabu's is a record shop in Cape Town. The interior is a work of my imagination. Next time I'm in CT, I'll be sure to visit.

In writing *Ultramarine*, I've appreciated and valued: Barbara Turner-Vesselago's approach to writing (Freefall writing); Ben Evans, The Literary Consultancy (TLC) and Vicki Heath-Silk. In addition, the writing of *Ultramarine* would have been a different experience without my much-loved and indispensable far flung Beta readers—Cate Gray, Amanda Ferguson and Lou Richards.

My thanks also to the Bridport short story competition, the Aurora prize for writing, Bibliophone, Lorian Hemingway short story competition and the Tillie Olsen short story award—my success with these competitions was a springboard for this collection.

Many moons ago, when I was completing my Masters, Dr Chris Seeley told me I must have stories to write. I thank her for setting me on this path. She is still sorely missed by many.

I would like to acknowledge the Eora Nation who are the traditional custodians of the land in which my story Jacaranda tree is set. I would also like to pay respect to the Elders both past, present and emerging, of the Eora Nation and extend that respect to other Aboriginal people.

And lastly to friends and my family who have stood quietly on the side lines, specifically and most dearly, Alan, Louisa and Max, my thanks.

Ingram Content Group UK Ltd.
Milton Keynes UK
UKHW010023040723
424490UK00005B/297

9 781788 649643